MW00748180

ERIS

ERIS

LARRY GAUDET

Copyright © Larry Gaudet, 2024

All rights reserved. No part of this publication may be reproduced, stored in a retrieval system, or transmitted in any form or by any means, electronic, mechanical, photocopying, recording, or otherwise (except for brief passages for purpose of review) without the prior permission of Dundurn Press. Permission to photocopy should be requested from Access Copyright.

All characters in this work are fictitious. Any resemblance to real persons, living or dead, is purely coincidental.

Publisher: Kwame Scott Fraser | Acquiring editor: Russell Smith
Cover designer: Laura Boyle
Cover image: woman: istock/Diamond Dogs; texture: istock.com/gadost

Library and Archives Canada Cataloguing in Publication

Title: Eris / Larry Gaudet.
Names: Gaudet, Larry, author.
Identifiers: Canadiana (print) 20230514219 | Canadiana (ebook) 20230514227 | ISBN 9781459753631 (softcover) | ISBN 9781459753648 (PDF) | ISBN 9781459753655 (EPUB)
Subjects: LCGFT: Thrillers (Fiction) | LCGFT: Novels.
Classification: LCC PS8563.A824 E75 2024 | DDC C813/.54—dc23

We acknowledge the support of the Canada Council for the Arts and the Ontario Arts Council for our publishing program. We also acknowledge the financial support of the Government of Ontario, through the Ontario Book Publishing Tax Credit and Ontario Creates, and the Government of Canada.

Care has been taken to trace the ownership of copyright material used in this book. The author and the publisher welcome any information enabling them to rectify any references or credits in subsequent editions.

The publisher is not responsible for websites or their content unless they are owned by the publisher.

Printed and bound in Canada.

Rare Machines, an imprint of Dundurn Press
1382 Queen Street East
Toronto, Ontario, Canada M4L 1C9
dundurn.com, @dundurnpress

For Alison and our sons, Jackson and Theo,
and the memory of my father-in-law, Stan Smith

Don

The boy has a deep feel for the game. A hacker malevolence tweaks everything he touches. He plays with the blind confidence of an oracle, as if he were born to a special destiny. His command of game glitches and cheat tactics is uncanny. For hours at a time, every day, he forges ahead, minute by billing minute, sometimes going all night and past dawn. When does he eat? Sleep? When does he dream — and of what?

His handle is T-Redeem.

Already, today, he's accomplished so much. He spent a whack of credits on carbon scrubbers for cleaning up Chinese airspace polluted by coal power plants. He bankrolled a Brazilian group — apparently, high schoolers in a *favela* near Rio — to reforest a tract of rainforest. In the Canadian sector, he opened discussions with gamers on a virtual Indigenous reserve. Their conversation was in a coded slang, but it's clear they're planning a terrorist intervention at the Athabasca oil sands simulation.

All this and more, woven into a tapestry of gaming brilliance. He's realized this by now, but Greenhouse was designed so that only millions of paid player transactions over decades would cause a meaningful drop in temperature sufficient to forestall disaster in the game's virtual climate. If the virtual temperature does rise too high, or too quickly, the game itself will destruct, orphaning players all over the planet. That threat, as unreal or absurd as it sounds, is a pillar of our player engagement and corporate billing model. We want players to believe they're contributing to a goal larger than themselves.

The few staffers left on my team have been instructed to keep everyone and everything away from me for now, excluding Bai Jun, my Chinese successor as CEO of Greenhouse. Here, in the wilderness of Vancouver Island, in the mountains, in a well-appointed grouping of cottages disguised to look like old shacks, I'm on sabbatical.

I've had a career, been there, done that, taken names, kicked ass, delivered results, and, best of all, engineered the takeover that brought us into the deep pockets of a Chinese hedge fund that will grow the business for a long time to come.

I spend too much time monitoring the boy's activity in the game, but it's generally an enjoyable pastime. I designed the game. I gave it life. I nursed it from prototype through launch and into mass deployment that now delivers obscene profits internationally. I have also, genetically speaking, participated in designing the boy.

I'm his father.

This week he's with me, away from his mother — well, his lanky fifteen-year-old body is with me. To say we're bonding or reconnecting is a stretch. He games when awake. I watch him game when I'm awake, impatiently waiting for another moment when it's possible that words might, in a physical space, in real time, pass between us.

On his last bio-break:

"Dad, why did you do it?"

"Do what?"

"Greenhouse."

"Create it?"

"Love it, Dad. More than you loved me and Mum."

"I am sorry you see things like that," I say after a gloomy pause. "Son, I was trying to do something good. To get people active. To educate — no, to *engage* them in something important. And a good way to do that these days is through games."

"It's only a game, Dad."

Then he's gone again, back into the game, his controller agitating in micro-movements — same with the headset. He likes to yank my chain, for sure. On some level, he repels me with his devotion to the game, his lack of interest in anything else.

As I watch over him while working on my financial portfolio, I notice that at times he appears to hold his breath for too long. Sometimes, when he exhales, it comes out as a melodramatic sigh. After an hour of passive observation, I can't resist going into the game to see what he's up to. The classic helicopter-parent move.

He's embroiled in a small green infill project where, with the assistance of some local gamer activists, he's demolishing a public housing project that our designers built with the usual elements: drugs, gangs, guns, violence. It's a pixelated, interactive canvas of urban danger and depravity. The old buildings (and gangs) are all gone now, and in their place something new is rising. A cohort of gamers, led by my son, is actively earning game credits by working together to create an organic urban farm. While that's in progress, they take most of their newly earned credits and allocate them to poorer members to help them buy condos near the farm. We call this holistic redistribution: First, you earn credits by doing something environmentally sustainable and then you redistribute a percentage to those most in need. This is one of several Robin Hood dynamics of the game, an idea that I worked up from my superficial reading of Marx. I'm not sure what Marx would make of the transaction fees we charge members to facilitate these wealth exchanges, not to mention the monthly subscription fees to remain active players. But these fees allow the company to keep investing in the entertainment quality of the game for the benefit of all members — but also, importantly, to provide sufficient profit margins to keep shareholders happy. I'm proud of my son's work here, except for one thing: He's demolishing the neighbourhood where I grew up.

I request a private chat. I get an automated reply that tells me he's out of touch. I respect his concentration in the game, his focus. I'm sure his ADHD meds are of some value here. The kid only very rarely snacks or takes bathroom breaks while in the game and, given that he's loudly passing gas every couple of minutes and squirming in his console, I just wish he'd listen to his body more.

T-Redeem: Dad, what's up?

GM001: It's starting to look pretty good.

T-Redeem: Thanks. So you're not mad, what I'm doing here.

GM001: Why would I be?

T-Redeem: Come on, you shut me down here always.

GM001: Stopped that a while ago.

T-Redeem: Mum made you stop.

That isn't totally true. I was encouraged, not formally ordered, by his mother and her therapist, to let him express his resentments as the divorce got real. Yet, it's unnerving to have him apply his unique gifts to remake the place where I grew up.

I mentioned this to our corporate psychologist when we were updating my video diary together. She warned me it's easy to stroke my ego by thinking this is a form of Oedipal acting out. She cautioned me not to jump to conclusions. Maybe so, but he isn't destroying his mother's old neighbourhood, which is a much more environmentally degraded suburban setting of McMansions, shopping malls, and epic parking lots.

GM001: This is the only place you want to talk, I guess.
T-Redeem: What?
GM001: Well?
T-Redeem: It's the only place you listen, lol.

The game is really no place for a father to speak to a son who, in this world, is something like a teen warrior-king. As the principal game designer, I have access to tools to control his behaviour here. I have the power to destroy or infiltrate the T-Redeem persona he's created. His mother recently suggested this, telling me that he spends so much time here he's in danger of failing his last year of high school. True, I can wipe his credit balance with a single keystroke. I can't bring myself to do that, for two reasons. One, he'd find a way to get or steal credits somewhere and fairly easily find his way back into the game by buying a fake avatar from one of the many resellers out there. Two, the proud father in me is, I'll admit, stoked by his tactical brilliance.

T-Redeem advises me by chat that he's launching an operation that will prevent him from responding for some time. A common tuning-out tactic. I look up from my screen and I'm tempted to cuff him out of his trance. But he's here for only a week that's ending today, and I don't want him leaving angry at me. His new operation is making credits available to help locals buy seed stock for the urban farm in my old neighbourhood. Problem is, they can't agree on what they want grown there. T-Redeem issues an ultimatum: a decision by end of day or he'll take back the credits, which causes outraged chatter from players who feel this should take weeks, and involve some kind of vote, or referendum. Like a lot of top players his age, the democratic instinct is far from fully developed. He thrives on exploiting power imbalances.

I log out.

"Hey, you, it's time, it's enough," I say, mussing his hair.

"What? Just a minute, okay."

"Your car's going to be here any minute now."

"Sure."

"Now — I mean *now*," I say with parental emphasis.

T-Redeem logs out and becomes Tony again, muttering resentfully while rubbing his right wrist. Repetitive stress, so young. He knows enough to hide the ailment from his mother. She has put limits on his gaming before and expects me to do the same. I'm not so good at monitoring. But I did arrange for acupuncture treatments, which, he says, have made the discomfort manageable.

Silently, I watch him dismantle and pack his console into the titanium travel cases I gave him for his last birthday. Tony should have been an athletic kid, with his body type. Sadly, he's starting to acquire that post-physicality vibe. Maybe I'm just seeing things that are more a reflection of my fears, as all parents do. Maybe it's just adolescence kicking in, a natural but temporary awkwardness. But I think I can see the dreaded shoulder hunch you get from all those hours at the screens.

We go out into the morning haze, a golden fog thinning fast, the air starting to warm up after the cold overnight rain. We hand his luggage over to the driver.

I watch the Range Rover disappear around the bend. Before I head back in, I ask myself whether I can ever fully retreat from the life I've made for myself. I'm a game designer, a global visionary in the immersive arts. I will feed in revenue streams far into the future, with the potential to shape the lives of my grandchildren and theirs, too. Grandchildren? Who knows what's ahead for my son? Will he lead a life that produces off-spring? It all seems so preposterous, so unlikely.

I can't imagine his life outside the game.

At dawn the next day, my time, I get an alert that he's back in the game, presumably from his mother's condo in Toronto. I enter the game while he's orchestrating a macabre gesture in symbolic violence. The scenario features three vultures feasting on the remains of about a dozen Corporates. T-Redeem has managed to insert audio clips into each corpse of the dead personas, killed by him in skirmishes around his projects. As the vultures snuffle into the entrails of the avatars in question, you hear screams and pleas to stop, please, stop, but the screams stop only after the remains are totally consumed.

Brilliant, T-Redeem.

Next, I follow him to a nature preserve — not rendered as well as it should have been — in a mountainous stretch of Western Iberia, largely abandoned by humans in the real world. T-Redeem materializes there to meet up with the activists of a rewilding co-operative who are introducing a generation of virtual wild horses built up from an ancient Spanish breed. I went there, the real place, during a backpacking trip on my own, and it made a real impression on me. Unfortunately for the gamers, the virtual experience is nothing like what I recall. All the rich colours of the fauna, the flavours of green and violet, the orange-red soil after a rain: all this riotous interplay just looks cheesy on a screen or in an immersive environment.

In my stalking, mostly I lurk invisibly. T-Redeem acts as if I'm not there, but he knows I am, or expects me to be. We discussed this. It's hard to say how my presence affects his behaviour, but I'm inclined to believe it leads to larger, more dramatic gestures.

Tony

Amazing how good McDonald's fries are right out of the fryer, salted and oily hot. No need to sugar them up with ketchup. Amazing how bad they are cold, though — all fucking wrinkly, like chewing on worms. Mum would go ballistic if she found out where I'm eating. I hate to admit it, but fast food is crap when that's all you eat.

Eris says I should stick to the McDonald's at the mall, using the burner debit card she left for me under the garbage bin in the park next to Mum's building. She says the transactions go into some kind of digital black hole in the global payment reconciliation network, making it impossible to track me — or her.

Eris and I have been talking for months in the game, but today's the first time we're meeting in person, now that I've left home. For all I know, Eris might be a dude. She won't do video or send photos or anything to clue me in on what she looks like. I tried everything to get a picture of her. With girls my age, I've gotten pretty good at getting them naked on the screen. My hit rate is way better than all my guy friends, for sure. But nothing has worked with Eris. She's all business in the game. She's at my level, certainly, and more powerful in some ways, which is freaky. As good as my dad — better, even.

She's just texted me to say there's a cargo van making its way here to pick me up and take me to this safe house where supposedly we'll get down to work.

It's seriously hot outside, the kind of day where — even if it's sunny and the sky shines blue — everything at ground level looks filthy: the cars, the road, the people. Across the street from the mall are townhouses, all fronted up with this fake stone, all squeezed together as if there's no space out here, which, really, that's all there is. I sound like my dad. He can't go out to the mall without getting a massive headache. He always waited for us in the car, staring into his fucking phone while Mum did the shopping, which drove her nuts when they were married.

It's weird in the world outside the game. I have a hard time judging distances, especially on the sidewalk, where I keep bumping into people. I keep forgetting to move my body, using only my hands to avoid collisions. Also, visually, it's not like looking into a screen, where you control everything, focusing on what you want and when. Out here, your eyes have to work harder. Nothing seems stable even when you do focus on something. I guess it's the sun and clouds changing the light. Still, it's tiring.

And there it is, the van, driving into the back of the mostly empty parking lot. Windowless except for the silver windshield you can't see through.

I slip out of McDonald's, my gaze swivelling here and there, worried someone will recognize me, which is foolish, as we're two hours from downtown. I make my way to the idling van where the side doors slide open, just as a voice call comes in.

Eris: Just get in.

It's a woman's voice, smooth, yeah, not a girl my age, no fucking way.

There's no one in the van. It's a self-driving vehicle. Cool. The place is kitted out with a futon and the craziest console rig I've ever seen: three screens and a rack of headsets that look insane. Heavy-duty, aftermarket custom stuff. There's a beer fridge off to the side and, as I settle in, the woman's voice comes into my buds again, telling me the kombucha blends were mixed especially for me. She says it's nothing strong, just some kind of futuristic ADHD meds blended with an anxiety reducer. She promised me a better mix than I'm used to, all to help me take my game to the next level.

Eris: Here you are, T-Redeem. How do you feel?

T-Redeem: I'm fucking scared, actually. You've never said where we're going. And, like, where are you?

Eris: We'll answer that all soon enough.

T-Redeem: I thought we were going to meet with the others?

Eris: For the next several hours, the van will be doing evasive manoeuvres. So there'll be a lot of doubling back and forth, as well as moving through the faraday zones we've set up to *invisiblize* the van, as best we can, before we lock in your destination.

T-Redeem: Invisiblize. Is that, like, a word?

As soon as I settle onto the futon, I get pinged with an encrypted channel on my phone with a cover message saying to use it, only once, for texting my parents. I'm advised the message will flow through Eris, who will secure it before putting it across the network. If this is supposed to notify my parents, okay, let's get it over with.

There's a part of me that wants to go home right now.

Eris says doubts are good. Her instructions: Be careful; don't reveal where you are or where you were picked up, what you're doing. And if I say something I shouldn't, she says, she'll fix that before sending it on to Mum and Dad.

> Mum, Dad, am okay. I can't tell you where
> I am. I am doing something that is important to the world, that is all I can say.
> I am trying to eat good so don't worry.
> I am joining the fight. Life is not a game
> but you have to play it like a game and I
> am going to do good even if it does not
> look like that, your son love

I hit send, but nothing happens, not for several minutes. Then Eris texts me to say she'll pass on any messages she gets back.

I am pretty sure Eris is real. But there are moments when she — if she is a she — does sound like an AI. I was drawn to Eris because she can really game. Does shit in Greenhouse that is, in theory, totally impossible, except for an elite gamemaster like my dad. He's taught me a lot about game cheats. Eris taught me other things, like about the world, sending me all those docs on the history of revolution, on capitalism, on colonialism, corporate evil, and tons of history crap I never heard about at school. Our conversations make me think about my gaming, and how it might be put to better use, how I might help save the world from people like my father.

Eris says she doesn't want me to hate my dad.

But she wants me to ruin what he has created. To destroy Greenhouse.

I once asked her, Why don't you just fucking do it yourself?

She laughed, like a seriously weird laugh, then said, You might not understand this now, and it's something of a cliché, but it's much better if you, his son, do it.

Sometimes it's hard when I think of my parents hurting because of what I'm about to do. I know one day I'll get caught, go to jail, or die.

I know some will think I'm just some kind of terrorist.

It's pretty weird to be so good at something I need to destroy.

I just want to create a better world. Not live in the one given to me by my parents. Not waste my time living in a society that exploits people, makes them stupider. I always thought gaming made me smarter, but Eris pointed out that I'm smart only in the game, not outside it. Can't disagree. I try not to think about how angry my dad will be. He'll make life miserable for everybody until he takes down Eris and whoever else is in her group. Mum doesn't panic but I don't want to think about what's going on in her head.

Eris says I'm gifted. I don't like the word and told her, Stop it. I just got so sick of hearing it at school. All these gifted kids, gifted programs. Sometimes gifted kids are basically the special-needs types, like on the spectrum, and what I guess they now call neurodiverse. Is that me? Hard to say. Anyway, you never know what to call anyone anymore. Sometimes it's just for geeks like me who play video games, and don't do sports or homework. I'll say this for my dad: He too hates that "gifted" talk. Says the parents of these kids are the worst. Going on about how smart their kids are because of tests that test only how good you are at doing tests. He says shit like that all the time and really pisses people off. Maybe that's why he doesn't have any good friends, only people who work for him.

In the van, we're moving at a speed that says "highway" to me.

The juice blends are stronger than I was told.

I feel myself drifting off —

Lily

I can't stop myself from attacking Don on our video call about how he handled our son's recent visit. Tony says he played Greenhouse non-stop the entire week.

"Is there any other subject but my failures as a father?" he asks. "By the way, where is the young man as we speak?"

"Staying at a friend's house this weekend, a classmate, a nice boy. They'll play video games until they drop. Eat too much popcorn."

"I thought video games went against the state religion at the condo."

"What am I supposed to do? Lock up him and the games twenty-four–seven?"

"You sure girls aren't involved?"

"Don," I say, sarcastically. "He's not you. The lying is not quite as advanced, yet."

I lean back from the screen, arms folded. I wonder what he sees. I still find myself posing for him. My red hair is pulled into a tight bun, the makeup emphasizing my mouth and blue eyes, the freckles buried in my new filters.

I've not forgotten how my skin goosebumped to his touch writing itself across my body. But all I'm left with are memories — many of them bad. The divorce got ugly. It's a few years ago now but we both said terrible things. In an angry moment after the courts gave me custody, he said there'd be payback.

Payback?

As he talks — or, rather, explains himself without convincing me — I text him a picture of himself at a recent gamer conference, culled from a tabloid, the Caribbean and palm trees behind him. On each arm, a young woman in a skimpy bikini.

"I hardly remember the moment," he says, his turn to lean away.

"It's not jealousy, I can assure you. It's my son. And what he thinks of you. He googles you, you know."

"Our son, you mean."

"Our son — fine."

"What our son thinks is very little about his father."

"That's not true, but would you blame him if that's how he felt?"

"Those girls are not groupies —"

"Right. They're designers, on your team, whatever."

"It was a sales conference. They're in sales. Or marketing, maybe. I am supposed to be nice to people like this."

He had groupies. All serious game designers do, apparently. The investigators said he slept with only a couple of them during our marriage.

You only ever really know about ten percent of what's going on in people's minds. That's what my therapist told me prior to me kicking Don out.

He seems to lose interest in our conversation, judging by the frequency of his gaze wandering to an upper corner of the screen, along with the blank look on his face.

"So," I say, too abruptly, probably. "Who has your attention over there?"

Keyboard clicks.

It takes him a few seconds to respond.

"It's work, always work — sorry."

"I thought you had taken a sabbatical, or were about to retire."

When I met him all those years ago, he was deep into producing the game that made his name, Greenhouse. I was on track for tenure in the Environmental Studies department at MIT while making great consulting money on the side, hooking up with small companies like Don's through a Boston venture capitalist. At times I traded my talent for equity, which turned out to be lucrative when I got share options in Don's company before it went public. I did a lot of work gathering data inputs on the environmental conditions in many of the first-generation game landscapes that made Greenhouse so popular right out of the gate. But after fifteen years at home playing Tiger Mum, my career prospects aren't on the fast track anymore. I'm fine with that. I've landed a nice, non-tenured lecturing gig that keeps me engaged with developments in my field. It leaves just enough time to be around for Tony, who, of course, right now, wants to spend as little time as possible with his mother and as much time as possible in his father's game.

Don clicks away as if I'm not there. To him I'm no more than a data stream that can be turned on or off, reduced in size with a click, pushed to a corner of the screen, incidental to the moment, like grit in the eye, a ghostly annoyance. It wouldn't surprise me if he were sexting someone — it's happened before, in the failing stages of our marriage. I can't remember who it was, either the celebrity DJ or the marketing guru who runs the non-profit, both full of themselves, both all over Instagram with daily updates on how their booty or tits are somehow delaying the impact of gravity and time.

The truth: The occasional unseemly pang of jealousy aside, I don't want him back.

"Hey," I finally say, "can you give me your full attention?"

"I'm sorry."

"The shit you throw my way. Really."

In silence, he seethes at me, then drops off.

He wasn't an obvious choice for a husband, never mind the father of a child, so awkward and intense, always knotted up by this hunger to transform every waking moment — his every insight or intuition and those in the air around him — into material for the landscapes and capabilities of his games. Emotionally stunted? He felt life deeply, yes, but couldn't connect himself easily or intuitively to me or to others, ever. Was it his native wiring, the chemistry of the man, his energy profile? The ludicrous fact of being parentless at sixteen? What mix of what turned him into him?

I remember that Sunday morning after our first night together, after a second bout of clumsily enjoyable sex, feeling guilty at a pub brunch because of undone prep work for my seminar, nursing the Bloody Mary that I didn't need. I listened to him for two solid hours about some game strategy he was noodling on. He was convinced he was unlocking secrets in the human condition that only he knew existed. He reminded me of a missionary, malnourished or alienated in some important aspect of himself, bewildered in a hostile land, seeking converts one by one — not so much by the logic or the utility of his arguments, but through the sneaky allure of his loneliness.

I was the pretty and sporty girl with upward mobility away from the suburban middle class, a princess in the palace of smarty-pants ambition. First place came naturally. I was confident as only a private-school girl on scholarship can be. The men came in waves, on bended knees. A few women, too. There were so many dating choices when I went into the world with my degrees and dreams. There were corporate lawyers and investment bankers, not to mention a platoon of potential soulmates from my own field, a scientist here, a professor there, an eco-policy wonk over there.

What got me was his persistence, showing up where he wasn't expected or even welcomed, barging into my network of aspirations, elbowing the competition away. He had no manners — or none that held him back. He wanted me so badly. If not always for my body, then for my smarts. The sex was okay, if not mind-blowing as it had been with my first love, the bad boy from Bogotá, who skillfully pretended he cared about the Antarctic ice sheet, goofing off on his father's money for a doctorate he'd never finish (but, Lord, he knew how to undress a woman after riding her around on a Harley).

What was it about Don that I fell in love with? It must have been his now-incredible belief that he could change the world for the better with Greenhouse. It was only a game, he conceded — of course it was only that. Yet he argued me blue in the face that games fulfill our hard-wired need to be entertained as a methodology for developing new survival strategies. Lord, some messed-up misreading of Darwin, about whom I'm sure he never read more than a Wikipedia entry. A video game changing the world? Insane belief, but attractively so at the time, because it was an affront to my own pragmatic approach to life and to my work, which had nothing to do with games but rather with empirically correct data-gathering methodologies. Also, no question, I was attracted to his potential to make real money with Greenhouse, which in fact happened.

Don's ideological gambit — or delusion — wore thin over time as I watched my son and his friends slouching their lives away, playing the game. My disgust flowered. Self-disgust, mainly. That type of disillusionment in a marriage doesn't hide well. It crackles in a thousand unstated resentments and subtle put-downs. Could I blame him for bedding a few starfucker groupies, which certainly didn't qualify as affairs of the heart? Even the nanny, although technically Big Sister had quit before that happened. He was incapable of understanding that an emotional deception would have been much worse.

At one time I wanted to grow with him, but the better he got at what he did, the more successful he was, the more diminished he appeared to me. He was moving backward, devolving to some earlier stage of himself. Maybe he felt that to speak to teenaged boys, he needed to become one again? Maybe what he needed to say in his work was incompatible with adult perspectives? I asked myself all the *maybe* questions over and over, but the truth is that I moved on from him as soon as I could.

Jun

The morning is temperate, the trees still dripping from last night's rain, the light soft and warm, a reminder that the actual — not the digital — world is what nourishes us best. A stranger watching us could easily surmise we're two good friends out for a stroll. Our voices are cordial in their mingling. Every gesture between us is coded in culturally appropriate modes of respectful conduct. In truth, there's only a veneer of civility in play as we meander along a winding stone path in the hillside grove near the village of Longjing, a short drive from Hangzhou, the prosperous capital of Zhejiang province.

He's come here in the official capacity of inspector from the Central Committee of Discipline Inspection. A portly man, my age. His belly spreads like a waterfall over his trousers, disguising a signifier of his affluence and influence with Party leaders: a Gucci crocodile belt. Around his shoulders there's a cashmere scarf embroidered with a herringbone motif, Italian made. Flaunting these accessories indicates that he supplements his Party salary with black-market activity. It's not exactly a hint for a bribe. More that he'd like to befriend me, enter my world, and, over time, benefit in some way. Perhaps be given the right to buy discounted shares in one of my companies, or a stake in offshore real estate — a condominium or hotel in Vancouver or Sydney or Los Angeles, where many of us have significant assets we've managed to extract from the mainland.

Now and then we stray off the path to explore the rock caves hidden in the trees. Some have walls carved with ancient characters and hold embedded relief statues of Buddha, the ground inside spattered in red candle wax from votive rituals. Don Barton's creative teams constructed at least one Greenhouse landscape that contains hiding places that look like these caves, which I'm certain he did to impress me and my backers during the courtship phase before our acquisition. This was his way of saying, *There's a good cultural fit here* ... or, more arrogantly, *I understand you and China, too.*

Not far ahead of us in the valley, in Longjing proper, on a plateau of foothills above the other buildings in the vicinity, is a two-storeyed concrete box roofed with a pagoda in galvanized steel. My favourite home. It has wonderful views of the fields all around us, the tea bushes resolving as undulating lines across the mountainous green.

"This is a rich area now," I say to the inspector. "Even at the worst of times, the green Dragon Well tea here was always prized. Everyone from China wants to come here with their families. It is an important part of our heritage. The little we remember."

"And you are a rich man today," the inspector offers.

At last on my patio, we sit at a wooden table that has been set with a bowl of sunflower seeds and two glasses layered in green tea leaves. The old woman, Wen, is suddenly present, pouring steaming water into our glasses from a ceramic Thermos. She bows wordlessly as she retreats. Wen has been with us from very far back, my father's sister, never married, not intellectually gifted, but so often a comfort to me in those difficult years. My daughter's favourite person. I can only dream of having a relationship with my daughter as she has with my aunt.

After we settle in with our tea, the inspector says, "I know your parents were teachers, but when things became difficult, they were sent to work here. Correct? It could have been so much worse. They could have been sent into the interior, where it was much more difficult and cruel on intellectuals."

"My parents were executed for crimes they did not commit. By local cadres."

"Forgive my ignorance. That was not in the file."

"There is more forgotten here than we remember."

He cracks into a sunflower seed, spitting the shell into his palm. I wonder what he sees, looking at me. I suspect he knows there is a man behind this suit who isn't afraid of much, certainly not him. A man who has political friends in the highest places.

"I am not sure why I came back here." I shrug. "For years I worked these fields with my sister after my parents were murdered. Slaves, we were. The old woman who served us tea — my aunt. Without her, we would have died. Maybe I am drawn back to the source of my pain as a man. That sounds like bullshit, yes?"

And he laughs, mouth wide open, exposing the crude dental work that speaks to his own tough upbringing. "We all have these stories," he says. "But pain when it is understood, and respected, can benefit us, help us make better choices."

We keep talking like this, in clichéd abstractions and analogies, only hinting at the more difficult realities or possibilities underneath the safety of our uncreative wordplay.

To an American or European, this conversation would puzzle. On the one hand, my new friend is here to advise me of the possibility that Greenhouse, and our leadership team, and myself especially, may be subject to an anti-corruption investigation after the next Congress, all depending on shifts in leadership and our standing with the ascendant leaders. On the other, seeded within this warning, is a non-stop stream of compliments about my business acumen, how I'm an inspirational model for all Chinese entrepreneurs and, in his opinion, an incorruptible pillar of the country's corporate elite. This is normal Chinese talk from a Party loyalist.

"Are you aware the Pudong group in Shanghai is operational in Greenhouse?" he asks offhandedly, assuming this surprises me. It doesn't. He's talking about the military's cyberwarfare unit now subject to American indictments for intellectual property theft and hacking mayhem worldwide in many governments and corporations.

"If they are in there," I say politely, "then they're only playing the game. Nothing else. Our Security team has assured me that our core game systems are still completely secure, operating without interference or compromise."

"That's the situation today," he replies, equally politely. "But I've heard they would like more, shall we say, meaningful access to your platform. This is to ensure the game is not used in any way to harm our national interests. There are fifteen million Chinese game-players of the forty or fifty million in total. Surely you can see the merit of Party oversight."

So there it is: He wants us to grant Pudong unlimited systems access to the game.

"I understand the patriotic objective," I say, more sternly than I should have. "But surely you recognize that, as a corporate entity, Greenhouse is traded on all the major international exchanges. And while more and more of the company's leadership and operations are in China, we are still regulated as an American public company."

"You recognize the risks of non-co-operation."

"You must know that I've already been approached by actors within the American intelligence community about giving them access to our systems so they can assess any cyberwarfare risks to American security. An offer I've declined."

"Yes, but I've heard the Americans are now working with the Pudong group. Unusual but verifiable. They share a belief that a non-state cyber-actor is — or will soon be — inside Greenhouse. And it is a group, there is reason to believe, that sponsors terrorism in both countries, potentially."

How true this is I don't currently know, but I do manage to say, "Is this just more fearmongering about the North Koreans? Lies about the Russians again?"

"I said genuine non-state actors," he replies evenly. "There is also some concern about the former CEO, Don Barton."

"That is an interesting matter."

"There is chatter he is associated with the hacking group of concern."

"We are talking about a *game*, my friend. Not a weapons system or electrical grid or Swiss bank account. I don't see why we can't disable these hackers on our own."

"There are bigger security concerns that may not yet be apparent to you."

Eris

In the windowless rear of our van, I hover over Tony in a state of mute interest that feels, perversely, maternal. It's the first time we're sharing physical presence. I'm curious about the boy our trolling unit in Greenhouse has reeled in. He's fifteen or sixteen, not quite handsome but soon will be. Right now he's not sleeping the happy sleep of the dead but of the drugged. Best of all, strategically, he's Don Barton's son. I've spent a few years trying to take Barton down. My associates were starting to think my obsession with him counterproductive. Maybe it was. But having his son in our clutches changes everything. It's a unique opportunity to accelerate the scaling of our impact globally.

Curled up on the futon in a fetal position, sweating in his hoodie, drool on his lips, he's vulnerable in a way that teases up a protective urge that was once central to everything I valued. The wallet beside him holds only a subway transfer and our burner debit card. As requested, he left behind everything that could identify him. No ID on him other than, obviously, his DNA.

I feel like a mother, but what kind of mother am I?

The drugs we use during a secure travel event have been known to cause adverse health reactions. Earlier I felt he was on the verge of convulsing, but his vitals for the past hour indicate he'll be fine, if groggy for the first hour after he comes to.

But it's not time yet to end his narcotized slumber. At the safe house, where I'm shortly scheduled for an action-approval session, we'll have to mist him with more pharmo before moving him up into the attic that will be his home until the action heats up. He won't be happy to wake up alone, but we'll keep him busy enough in the game, no question.

We move at the speed limit, sometimes a little below, sometimes above. We're trying to convey that there's an inconsistent, law-abiding human foot on the accelerator. We worry about things like how a lack of randomized speed variability can alert the surveillance algorithms out there. We're careful in our route selections to follow precisely what a mainstream app would serve up, no custom workarounds. The risk of unwanted attention is higher on the back roads that go through small towns, where it's surprising how nosy people can be. Better to hide in plain sight, a vehicular sheep in the expressway herd, although we do make detours to flush through our faraday zones, which are useful in confusing any tracking drones on twenty-four–seven loops.

We turn off onto a winding dirt road and bounce along for a few minutes until we come to an abrupt stop. The boy is trying but failing to emerge from wherever we've sent him. As I step outside, I hit the pharmo misting app while my senses confront cheery birdsong and the evening breeze, which carries an aroma of wetland dampness from deeper in the woods. In the clearing, past the in-ground security triggers, behind the apple orchard, stands the old farmhouse with the bunker beneath it. It was a gift from a patron, a tax-haven billionaire whom we still support with our digital weaponization tactics — mainly ransomware attacks on his company's Asian and European competitors. We've also laundered crypto for him and disguised some of his offshore stock-trading patterns so that the regulatory authorities have little idea what he's up to.

Some of our alliances are clearly deals with the devil but, as they say, you can't make an omelette without breaking a few eggs. We need lots of money to live up to our purpose. It's a sad irony, perhaps, that to beat our enemy, we have to be better at what they do. Globally, our volunteer talent pool can do just about anything good or bad to a network, device, or service built on mediating technology and digital connectivity.

Ends and means and everything in between!

Inside the house, in the library, there's a large screen next to a bookcase that oozes the musty smell of decaying paper. The screen is alive with CGIs of wilderness landscapes in constant mutation, at once manifesting as real or identifiable places in the world but also otherworldly, too. Somewhere in this mesmerizing visual mix, there's an altered voice waiting to speak to me. It's one of our newer operatives, who, our bootlegged AI advises us, is likely from the American Midwest and likely in his midthirties, his conversational references indicating either corporate training or an intelligence background or both. His team, his cell, which came to us recommended by our Chinese cell, has recently completed several actions of dramatically violent substance that have raised money we absolutely need to keep funding our actions.

"You've requested a meeting, so the floor is yours," I say.

"We have uncovered a new revenue-generating opportunity," the altered voice says. "We were approached by a potential client, a corporate interest, impressed that we took both Fox News and CNN off the air at the same time. Even more impressed that we actually terminated celebrity journalists at both channels, live on the air."

"If anything, it proves we're not partisan," I say. "An equal-opportunity terrorist for these polarized times." The joke doesn't land with any impact.

"The client is open to investing in a spectacular action that serves both our interests: to interfere with a public company operating in media spaces where the client would prefer to own a monopolistic position. We'll be compensated extremely well. They want the company's leadership, to put it plainly, taken out. And ideally for reasons and through actions that cannot be traced back to them, obviously."

"What market space?"

"Mainstream porn. The Pornhome network."

"That is fully on brand for us, agreed."

"Agreed."

"You consistently find these revenue-generating opportunities, so-called. It makes me wonder if you're in this for the money or the cause."

He doesn't take that bait, either.

After a brief silence, he tells me the crypto deposit has already been transferred to us. Significant money. More than we've ever seen from a client.

He says, "There's a very good symbolic and strategic benefit to the operation."

"We've had Pornhome on our short list for some time."

"If we proceed, we'll need assets."

I send him the secure, one-time link to our global asset team.

"One day, perhaps we'll be able to show our faces to one another," he says. "Or sit at a table for a real conversation."

An unusual thing to say. Most of the active teams in our volunteer matrix, including his (if indeed he is male), have opted for permanent anonymity, or what we call cellular isolation, concerned as we all are that one day we'll be infiltrated, terminated, or taken to prisons where human rights go to die. Cellular isolation, a common strategy among intelligence agencies and revolutionary groups, is typically employed to stop the infiltration of one cell from spreading to other cells. So far this has worked fine for us, but a movement built on disconnected cells is vulnerable in other ways to bad actors.

"As desirable as meeting you is, it's not likely," I say. "Very risky."

"There's a lot to learn about each other to further the cause."

"We'll see what the future holds."

"If we succeed this time, perhaps you'll invite us into the Greenhouse operation."

"You know about that?"

"Please, Eris. Even the paranoid and secretive engage in watercooler gossip."

"The Greenhouse team is in place."

"Understood. But it is the most ambitious program you've planned."

"If we need your team, you'll be notified."

"Noted."

And then he's gone.

As I walk back out to the van, I punch up a voice call with the cell leader who oversees our main indoctrination program somewhere on the continent. Where, specifically, I'm not privileged to know.

"Who's on deck?" I ask.

"We have two martyr assets at readiness stage."

"It came out in our last action that one of the martyrs had a long history of mental illness. That's unacceptable. It devalues us perception-wise as a bunch of crazies."

"That won't be a problem this time."

"Tell me more about the martyr profiles."

"One's a video gambling addict, in recovery for several years, perfectly sane, although there's very little left of his life. Wife gone, kids won't see him. Stage four cancer, too, more or less palliative. So he hits all our buttons."

"The other one?"

"She's a little too perfect — the *fit*, I mean. Trafficked out of Romania at sixteen. Did hardcore porn for years. Also, her videos on Pornhome are still active, which gives us the media spin we need to link cause and effect. Drugs came into the picture, of course. Cleaned up, but PTSD, yes. Obviously."

"PTSD is mental illness."

"Not if it isn't formally diagnosed, which we've been careful to verify. She's never seen a therapist or gone to a mental health clinic, not once. So in the event of any investigative coverage, I doubt the issue will surface."

"Do they understand the end game is their end, too?"

"Both appear to have gone deep into themselves, spiritually."

Back in the van, Tony is still out cold, as I expected he would be. I can't resist wiping his perspiring brow. Chills periodically surge through him. There's a part of me that wants to hold him, but of course I won't.

Not long after, our two contract minders on this assignment here open the rear doors and carry him away. Too roughly, yes, but their orders are to make it happen fast. You never know when a hunter or hiker will wander out of nowhere.

At times I struggle to believe it's me here.

Once we hit the highway, although I have work to do, I can't get anything done as the question keeps nagging me: What kind of mother am I?

Years before I committed to this life, I spent an afternoon wandering around the plaza of a famous museum that featured a towering bronze-and-steel sculpture of a spider, a pregnant female. Its eight legs projected out from its bulbous body, creating a canopied interior space within those tentacles that touched the ground like a circular medley of scalpels probing an incision site. As I studied this art-spider from all angles, walking around it, and then within it, I studied others doing the same. So many clearly saw or felt what I didn't: a menacing presence. What I saw in that spider was the beauty of maternal love as a violent necessity produced by evolutionary logic.

But what am I, right now, as a maternal figure?

A menace.

Two hours later, at the airport — not much more than a shack and a runway used by mining companies flying their people into the northern bush — I walk out to the waiting plane. The first of several bumpy rides to come. I'm not sure it's the best idea to leave Tony there, on his own, but he'll be kept busy when he wakes later today, doing what he loves most. Like many boys his age who tune into our messaging, he's defenceless, an innocent. But problematic. Where will his video game addiction lead? His porn habit? I want him to heal — but that journey, for him, is only beginning.

Don

It's like a drug, being here in the game again, active as more than a parental voyeur. Despite all the promises I've made to myself to abide by the spirit of the sabbatical, I've activated my omniscient gamemaster avatar, with good reason. A powerful new hacker group has surfaced. That alone isn't cause for excessive operational concern, as we've always known how to shut down hackers. What's different is that T-Redeem appears to be involved. Part of me is impressed. Like many parents, I'm too easily convinced that brains are inherited. True, he's very talented, but his data vitals suggest he's being counselled and technically supported by the hackers.

At the moment, we don't know who or where they are. We have a few cryptic message-board statements — screen graffiti, more or less — that the name of the group is "Eris." A search tells me it's the name of the Greek goddess of chaos. The goddess of entropy, a physicist might say. All we know right now is that they've infiltrated the game in ways that we don't yet understand. Happens now and then. Usually our counter-hacking teams quickly regain full transparency to our systems and reveal who's fucking with us. But this group is proving so much harder to deal with. The first reports out of Security aren't reassuring. The suggestion is that the hackers are just another cell among thousands in the hacktivist collective, SirVeil. Lazy analysis. We need forensically disciplined thinking. They could possibly be a rogue element in our customer support organizations, an inside job. That needs to be investigated. So far, we haven't seen traditional denial-of-service attacks on our network. Interestingly, they actually play the game, as characters, but with true gamemaster capabilities. They've been running wild for several days now. It's time to shut them down, except that the usual methods aren't yielding results.

Today's scenario is fascinating. Four hacker characters are present in one game sector, their avatars faceless bodies. Because of a surveillance upgrade I did on the boy's account a while back, which I suspect he doesn't know about, I can detect that he's here as one of them. Also in the scenario are five member characters who have been kidnapped by the hackers, trussed into nooses, up on gallows, rendered on an ice floe adrift on an Arctic-green sea. Polar bear corpses float all around them, their paws in the air. The characters are alive but unable to free themselves, crying out for help. All around them are the hackers, circling the gallows, hurling insults. It's creatively vindictive.

We architected the business model for randomly aggregating forms of group conflict. Generally, conflict is a good thing. It keeps people buying and redeeming credits, particularly in war situations when some members get seriously injured or killed en masse, which means they have to buy another life, or series of lives, to start playing again. Bottom line, we depend on anti-environmentalist shit disturbers to drive member engagement. Without them, the game isn't a game — just a bunch of preachers to the converted. Our marketing programs are designed to provide incentives for players to adopt negative, conflict-generating value sets, like what you encounter in the real world in the more malignant corporations, governments, and terrorist groups. Our latest numbers indicate that more than half our members profile negative. What we didn't plan for, however, was a conflict dynamic led by fully anonymous hackers. In our scenario planning, we raised the issue only superficially. *Mea culpa.*

Above the gallows, text appears, which is also transmitted right across the gaming ecosystem — much to Security's chagrin, I'm sure.

> *FOR CRIMES AGAINST GREENHOUSE, WE SENTENCE THESE COUNTER-SUSTAINABILITY HOOLIGANS TO GAME DEATH. THESE ENEMIES OF THE ENVIRONMENT CORRUPTED THE TRANSFER OF HEALING CREDITS TO THE OZONE LAYER ABOVE THE ARCTIC ZONE THROUGH INTERACTIONS TO FOIL THE EFFORTS OF THE HEROES OF THE ARCTIC DEMOCRATIC COLLECTIVE.*

Then the so-called criminals are hung, dropped through a trap door in the ice floe, their game characters actually killed. Brilliant! If these members want to keep playing, they'll have to buy credits to re-establish themselves.

There's a pause in the action.

I'm about to make myself visible and, if necessary, rope T-Redeem into my surveillance field. Before I can do that, the scene shifts to an endless brown desert. Very troubling. Shifts like that should be self-initiated by a member, or members acting together, but everyone in the polar sea space has been forcibly moved by the hackers.

I can't remember that ever happening before.

We're now in a lakebed, an endlessly toxic dust pit, swirling with storm winds. This is our unique simulation of the ruins of the Aral Sea in Uzbekistan, now only a fraction of its original size because of Soviet-era irrigation projects to divert the feeder rivers. We situated our game landscape circa 2003, at the worst of this environmental catastrophe, before the dam project was initiated to bring the lake back to life.

We really nailed the Aral Sea. Months of work getting the proper apocalyptic textures. We sweated the drama out big time.

The hackers have gone invisible.

Amazing that they can do that!

I approach a group of members on the ground, only to discover that I can use only voyeur mode here, not interact or affect the actions of anyone. This is the first time hackers have been able to do that, too.

The group on the ground is being used as forced labour. The members enslaved are all churning the lake bed, attempting to transform the land into something farmable, one metre at a time and consuming credits to do so. I dive into their data vitals: The hackers have programmed these members to a year of slave work before they're free to play again exclusively on their own terms, without restrictions. Again, this is good business. To turn the digital land into something arable, they'll all consume major credits. But the penalty here is too harsh. Our game rules stipulate that forced-labour activity must be limited to less than 5 percent of a member's credits. What's happening now is more like 100 or 200 percent. These members are either going to have to pony up a lot more money or quit the game. And our gamemasters and customer database people can't do anything about it.

The hacker problem is moving into territory we've never seen before. Our Security avatars are now chattering stupidly among themselves, bickering about who failed whom in this joke of a takedown. The argument is heated and I'm about to intervene and pull rank when I see that in the deep background of the scene there's a wonky grouping of pixels, a flutter of something happening there. And when I do a pixel biopsy, I discover the boy there, trying but not succeeding in staying hidden.

GM001: Having fun, son?

T-Redeem: Dad.

GM001: You're getting into trouble here.

T-Redeem: [no response]

GM001: So who are your friends?

T-Redeem: Why?

GM001: I will know soon, but I want you to tell me.

T-Redeem: [no response]

GM001: Now, son.

T-Redeem: Gamers, Dad.

GM001: Where are you right now?

T-Redeem: Here.

GM001: Where is this here, specifically?

T-Redeem: [no response]

GM001: Hey!

T-Redeem: We're Eris, Dad. Eris!

GM001: Where are you?

T-Redeem: Eris!

GM001: What?

T-Redeem: [user logged out]

Why did I ever have kids — this kid in particular?

I log out and call his mother.

"He'll be home from school soon," she says. "How serious is this?"

"He logged into the game right now from an IP address that we can't place, geographically. It keeps disguising itself. When did you last see him?"

"I told you. He spent the weekend with a friend and went to school from there."

"Have you heard him talk about Eris?"

"Eris?"

"Call me when he gets in."

Minutes after the call, I get an encrypted message from our Security VP in either Panama or the Seychelles, as I can never be sure where he's working from or whether he is she or they or some other pronoun. The hackers have just informed us through an incredibly complex and (for now) untraceable mode of communication, within the game, that my son has left home and joined their group voluntarily, that he's safe for now but can't be reached, and that contacting any law-enforcement agency or the media is not advisable, as the boy will be harmed as a consequence.

I'm advised to await further information.

I call Lily again to relay what I know. Right away, she dials us in to a call with the mother of the boy that Tony supposedly stayed with. Turns out, he was never there on the weekend.

After we drop the mother from the call, Lily instantly summons her unresolved anger toward me, although an outsider to our situation wouldn't hear explicit criticisms. But if you've ever been in a long-term relationship, you know that ugly emotions don't need words or gestures to drive the knife in, only a subtle shift in tone, or a longer-than-necessary pause. Perversely, while our concerns for our son are paramount in our exchange, at the same time we keep triggering each other with jibes about the other's character that are like old friends to us now, the traits we've both seen, etched in black ink, up on the therapist's whiteboard. At the top of Lily's list weren't my groupie infidelities, but my vocation, the game, Greenhouse. And today, who can blame her for thinking that? Our son is lost somewhere in the world I've given so much of myself to.

I need a corporate plane, so my next call is to Bai Jun, the Greenhouse CEO. To my surprise, he's on the plane that picks me up at the private terminal.

"We are in a form of dialogue with the hackers," he says. "Your son is safe."

"A form of dialogue?"

"The analysis indicates that the problem may be originating or operating in one of several international jurisdictions. They mutate their originating positions very fast."

"Could this be an internal problem? One of our own?"

"We are evaluating this possibility."

"Bai Jun, one option is to shut down the game and reconfigure all security procedures and interfaces. This will mean a short-term problem of consequence."

He shakes his head. "This was part of the scenario proposed to me by our crisis teams. This option is no longer available to us. The hackers are making it clear that we cannot stop and reboot the game."

"Or else what?"

"Something terrible will happen to your son."

I now intuit the corporate stress in the background and what the board is undoubtedly pressing on him. This man in a dark Savile Row suit, whom I consider a friend, is about my age but looks a fair bit older. He's impossible to read because of the thick lenses of his horn-rimmed glasses. Knowing him as I do, I'm certain strategies are being stress-tested for damage control and spin management. If hacker problems persist in the game, the fallout could be material, upsetting the business forecast for the year, maybe even completely derailing the company.

He leans forward, taking my hands in his, his head bent, allowing him to peer at me above his glasses. "I am a father of a daughter. We will do nothing to contribute to the potential for harm. You can trust me."

He's kept his word about everything since he took over the top job. He's allowed me to do what I want, like indulging myself in pet R&D projects in flaky areas of augmented reality and immersive gambling. He's freed up developers to build a few small environments, mostly to please myself, like my upgraded video diary archive. We are making stupid money in Asia, thanks mainly to Bai Jun and his Chinese leadership team. He doesn't fuck around. He really put the Silicon Valley money in its place, swooping in to buy a majority position in the company with his Party Princeling pals.

Then it hits me, hard — harder than anything I've ever felt.

"Bai Jun, do you think my son is still alive?"

Tony

I'm a little pissed that, for security reasons, as Eris put it, I gotta stay locked up in this attic in the middle of fucking nowhere. It's got everything I need to game non-stop. Even so, I didn't sign up for this. I thought we were going to hang out, do shit together.

I'm told again that will happen. But, for now, I need to be patient.

My assignment today is to penetrate Greenhouse databases and delete the accounts of members who are signed up as anti-environmental types, as Enemies of the Environment. It's a test, Eris tells me. A small but important one to determine whether in future I can take on bigger assignments.

T-Redeem: Let's roll.

Eris: Yes, but this is just a trial run, a test.

T-Redeem: Like, you don't think I can do this?

Eris: We've given you powers that require some learning.

T-Redeem: Yeah, sure.

No big fucking deal. The visual interface lets me steer into those databases like I'm racing a car through a seaside city.

Anybody who sees me in the game will briefly confront my avatar, until I tunnel under the city, which is where I'm told the member profiles are securely protected. The game's network security guys do not detect me.

T-Redeem: My dashboard has some really crazy stuff.

Eris: You're on your own right now.

I have about an hour to group together the members and delete their credits and accounts. All in all, there are nearly a hundred thousand members, and I instantly turn them to fucking digital dust. It's only a small percentage of the fifty million or so full-service members worldwide. But still. Just like that, with keyboard magic, I make them disappear from the Greenhouse world, along with all their credits.

I've done a lot of things within the game, but this is the first time I've hurt the game itself. My father will be unhappy. He's always so superior about his game, his baby, because it teaches kids about the environment, helps them get involved. Fuck, it just makes him rich. I'm not gonna say it isn't fun to destroy things. I do a lot of that myself in ways the game permits, but the more I listen to Eris, the more I realize that most of the kids in the game don't know jack shit about what's going on in the world. And I do know. I learned a lot last year with Mum on her trip with her students to the South Pole to see the changes in the ice. And then to Montana to see the melting glaciers. Eris said I have seen things, that I know things, that it's up to me to show my father the right way, the shining path forward. I am helping my father, she says. Helping him see the light.

Eris tells me it's time to retreat, like instantly.
But just as I do, my game interface gets eaten.
I jump over to a different console to see what's happening.

GM001: Son, where are you, with who, please?

I sign out and log into a different game sector.

GM001: You can't fool me with that trick.
T-Redeem: [no response]
GM001: Talk to me, please, son.

I log out again.
He must be really pissed.

Eris: You should not have gone back in a second time.
T-Redeem: How was I supposed to know my dad would see me?
Eris: Your reaction to evade, very good.
T-Redeem: What now!!!!!
Eris: You rest now after your mission — very well done, T-Redeem.

Two hours later, there's a billion stories on social media. We sort of got half-famous in fifteen minutes. We created big problems. Serious money got burned when we destroyed all those member accounts. The members who can't sign in to play the game are totally losing it on the blogs and vlogs. The people from my dad's company are saying the situation is under control, even as they say they don't know how the game got broken into and fucked up. I guess I did something. Can I ever go home now?

The next morning, after the sleep meds wear off, I'm on another mission.

It begins with a rumbling sound as my screens come alive in blue that slowly goes black, with pinpoints of distant light, as if I'm in outer space.

T-Redeem: The resolution here is unreal.

Outer space starts to change, turning into blue sky, a sunset sky, where a fat sun is slowly falling behind a mountain. I see a field, a sea of wheat, all swaying gold.

Sound quality is amazing. It really sounds like wheat swaying in the wind.

Eris: Do you know where you are?

T-Redeem: In the game somewhere.

Eris: Your mission begins in the wheat field.

T-Redeem: Sure, we burned a lot of these last year.

Eris: But only those with the genetically modified wheat.

T-Redeem: That's the point, isn't it?

Eris: See the farmhouse?

T-Redeem: Yup?

Eris: It holds the scenario modules source code.

T-Redeem: Like, the landscapes, communities, buildings, weather?

Eris: It's where your father protects his real children in life, his work.

T-Redeem: Like, this has gotta be like super protected.

Eris: Your persona has been updated with tools to get in there.

T-Redeem: Really.

Eris: Kill all characters on the way in.

T-Redeem: Then?

Eris: I will update you at the appropriate time.

T-Redeem: Let's go.

Eris: You will likely encounter your father.

T-Redeem: Shit, he'll kill me in the game.

Eris: We have given him a reason not to.

T-Redeem: Like?

Eris: We will kill you for real.

T-Redeem: What the fuck?

Eris: This is just to scare him. You are completely safe.

T-Redeem: Oh.

If my father taught me anything, it's not to be bullied by anyone, not to jump when people say jump, not even Eris. Yes, I'm scared. But I've got a brain. There'll be a dozen ways to work through the wheat field, from high aerial to stealth skimming and subterranean advances. It all depends on who's in the game, who's out to kill me, and how the weapons landscape actually manifests. Anything can and does happen.

T-Redeem: One more thing.

Eris: Yes.

T-Redeem: Did you ever, like, meet my dad IRL.

Eris: A question for another day, okay?

You don't think when you're in the game. You just *do*. If you take too much time to think, you're dead. Or kind of dead, until you buy back in. That's life. That's the game.

From the time I was old enough to use a console on my father's lap, I've been playing games. Games he made. Games he made by rebuilding the games of others, which Eris tells me is stealing something she calls intellectual property. When Mum went back to work, the nanny didn't care, either. Big Sister was sneaky. She lied to my parents about the hours I spent gaming. She even did my homework to help me out. We had a deal. I bought things for her online, using my dad's credit cards. I couldn't believe how fucking *absent* he was. It would have taken him ten minutes to figure out the scam if he really wanted to. But he was too busy.

My mother figured things out, eventually. I went through a difficult period with her. The consoles were locked up for a while. I was allowed to use them only in the living room with her there. I played along for a long time. Even pretended it was a good idea to activate all those parental controls. As if I didn't know how to get around them. I guess she began to trust me. I hope she will see that I am trying to do good, trying to do for real what she has not been able to do in her work. I am trying to make a good thing out of a bad habit.

I enter the wheat field at game speed. I'm obvious about it. No sense pretending they're not there in so many disguises.

As animals on the ground. Birds in the air. As hunters with plaid hats who can also fly. I totally respect a member who puts money into their disguises, into serious deception — like, in this situation, changing into the wheat itself or becoming dirt on the ground. Who knows what I'll run into? There's no element of surprise when you invade this kind of territory and those who think that should get out of the game and stick to doing things in real life.

It doesn't look like any wheat field I've ever seen. The terrain data tell me the game-builders were working from paintings by Vincent van Gogh, the guy who cut off his ear and then shot himself. I don't fucking get it. The field is bright but the theatre is sloppy. Not convincing. It just feels goopy to me. I far prefer battle landscapes that look real, totally precise, as if you could actually be there yourself. I'm equipped with enemy forensics that are not standard stuff that other members have. Apparently not even gamemasters have what I have, or so Eris says. But I don't trust anything or anyone, even Eris, when it comes to what we can do in theatre.

I push deep into the wheat, which is swimming in candy-sweet colours, all these yellows, reds, and greens. It's almost blinding. Like taking drugs or something. Not weed, but like something going around at a school dance.

Something's happening to my left — the first attack.

It's a haystack morphing into drone warriors, like right fucking now. I incinerate the whole platoon or squadron or whatever they are. What's left of the haystack now turns to mud. But it gets better: The mud rises up into something new, into these crazy-ass monsters, all with baby nukes drooling out of their mouths.

I go invisible.

Then I dive through the candy-wheat into black dirt, deep dirt, expecting to be attacked on contact. But nothing more, so I tunnel for a few seconds, then dive deeper and farther through the dirt where I suddenly hit open black air, a mine shaft and blue light up top, and that's where I decide to come up, no matter what's there, what's ready to kill me — except that, as I come up, I launch these cluster bombs that just blow all the blue out of the fucking sky, creating these fantastic colours and a huge gap where I can hover safely with an aerial view of the farmhouse.

As I rise, next to me, I feel my father. I know it's him because he's opened a message link in my scope grid. He's not visible, just an outline or something, a fucking *presence*. Even with shadow vision turned on, I can't see him. I just feel him nearby, hear his voice in my head. Typical gamemaster stuff on wicked steroids.

GM001: I just want to know if you're safe.

T-Redeem: Just doing my thing.

GM001: Are you being harmed?

T-Redeem: I am in the game, Dad, doing things.

GM001: I don't know what you're doing here.

T-Redeem: Here to do good, Dad.

That's when I sense another presence.

Eris: Tell your father more.

T-Redeem: What?

Eris: Tell him why you're here.

T-Redeem: Do I have to?

Fuck that.

There's a fire in my brain with these two grown-ups all over my ass. But I don't have time to worry. Or say much. But I won't take shit.

Out of the farmhouse — wow — come these huge cyborg locusts. Swarming. An upgrade on the typical game Protectors. I'm loaded with serious killing agent, a spray, which comes out the colour of orange juice. It's eating the locusts.

I keep moving forward.

Then everything freezes, as if the game needs a total reboot. Frozen everything.

I can't remember the game ever doing that before.

Eris: Your father has unusual powers.

T-Redeem: Can't move or do anything.

GM001: Let's have a chat here.

Eris: You should not have done that.

GM001: You don't make all the rules.

Eris: I warned you – your son's life.

GM001: I just want to see that he's okay.

Eris: Unfreeze everything – now.

The game being played here, fuck it. Grown-ups.

Then suddenly we're back in action. And my father's gone.

But when I try to pile-drive into the farmhouse, wow, I bounce the fuck back.

Eris: Your father has layered in a new security shield.

T-Redeem: Now what?

Eris: Retreat for now?

We fly together over a crater, then down, into a blackness that feels like there's light behind it. I have this sensation of falling and falling so fast I can hardly breathe.

We're being followed by Protector avatars from game Security.

Their searchlights are all over my ass, trying to bleach my avatar.

T-Redeem: They got me. They'll know where I am!

Eris: No they won't, we have a cloaking layer they haven't seen.

T-Redeem: Jesus, you guys are serious.

Suddenly I'm freed of light surveillance. My speed capacity has also just doubled.

We're in the fucking clear!

Although, I wish Eris had a more interesting avatar. She's just a grey fucking blob, as always. Some kind of cloud, I think. Sometimes the cloud is light, almost invisible, on the verge of disappearing. Other times, a storm cloud, bruised purple.

T-Redeem: Now what?

Eris: Up ahead there's a new surveillance filter just dropped in.

T-Redeem: That will fuck us for sure.

Eris: We will take care of that, trust me.

The filter is a sheet of venomous fog and, as we approach it, Eris releases a whole fucking payload of viper bombs. And I do the same.

We blow everything to fuck.
You can't beat the feeling of doing this.
And then I don't hear anything else.
I'm booted from the game!

T-Redeem: Holy crap.

Eris: I had to get you out. Your father was gaining ground.

Lily

When Don lands in Toronto near dawn and shows up at my condo soon after, I learn that he's been talking with Tony in the game. Stalking him.

Unbelievably, it's hard to get Don's undivided attention. He's taking calls one after the other from the company's PR people and the Security team in China. Apparently, our Tony was involved in destroying the member profiles of some hundred thousand members and news got out fast. As a result, the company's stock has wobbled today on many of the world's stock exchanges.

"Trust me, I don't give a shit about the stock," Don says. "I'm just trying to get as much info as I can about what our intrusion analysts are saying, and see if there's a way to track the kidnappers. I have to keep trying."

I really don't know what to think when Don tells me what Tony's up to in the game. He's lied to me about so many things in the past. All I know is that Tony isn't home, and not responding to his phone. So we wait and wait. For some reason, Don and I repeatedly drive past his school — why, I don't know. We inform the school he's in China with his father. His friends? I call the mothers of his besties without giving anything away, but learn nothing. We don't call the police. Don tells me the Security team says it's better to wait. Their reading of game data suggests that whoever's involved is trying to get to Don, perhaps seeking a ransom. Don tells me the hackers come in and out of focus within the game, but they're elusive.

And, currently, Tony is not among them. Where is he?

There are awful moments of hopeless hope, especially when I find myself pacing the lobby of the condo building, expecting Tony to come shuffling toward me, his sneakers untied, baseball cap rakishly backward, his backpack huge with the console and headsets he takes everywhere. But those hopeful moments come at longer and longer intervals and with increasingly painful letdowns each time. Late that afternoon, I fall asleep for a period that feels like forever but is likely no more than ten minutes, my head in Don's lap. He's stuck there, working his phone. At one point he rests his forearm on my head but retracts it as if catching himself in an embarrassing error.

Only once do I lose my composure while trying to feed Tina a pill for her heart condition. A now-elderly pug we brought home years ago as a puppy for our son, Tina is a portable affection device, a cuddly sack of white fur with the black Danish-pastry face, the sloppy-pink tongue. Tina is not herself, gagging up the pill twice. I yell at her. But then instantly reverse course, falling to my knees to coo out an apology. Then, in one motion, I pick her up, tickle her chin so that her mouth opens wide, flicking a pill down her throat.

That night, Don logs into the game in manic bursts of investigative panic, trying to connect with the boy and getting nothing — no location coordinates, no responses, nothing. As his interactions with Security increase, the insight-to-bullshit ratio goes to hell. The more talk there is, the less hopeful we become. Scenarios acquire ornamentation. A dialectical rhetoric has taken hold in our discussions with Security, all conducted by encrypted voice, no visuals. It produces alternatives, contingencies, and risk assessments, all from some pretty smart people. A terrible equilibrium has set in, a diminished expectation. It doesn't help that Security is mostly based in China. It makes discussion difficult across time zones and languages.

In the morning, after pulling an all-nighter, Don says there's nothing more to discuss or actually do for the moment, and he's decided it best to move into his old studio near the waterfront, where he can work more productively on finding Tony.

At the door, when he's leaving, we embrace, convulsively so. We're both crying and that's both comforting and alienating. As urgent as everything is, as connected as we are right now, as certain as we are that a drama must unfold toward bringing our boy back to us alive, it's weird to me that he feels he needs to go off on his own.

Shortly after Don leaves, the concierge downstairs tells me I have a visitor from Don's company who wants to come up. I vaguely remember the woman, a corporate psychologist, the kinder, gentler face of the Security group. I invite her up, thinking she's here to provide some trauma counselling for what we're going through. Fine, I could use it, for sure.

Sitting on my sofa, alertly turned toward me, she's the picture of burnished athleticism, softened up by the spectacle of her hair. The word is *tresses*: a glossy black mane of ringlets. Fantastic black hair against flawless white skin. Everything about her seems to be a dance between black and white. The creamy white silk blouse and the ivory pearls. The tight black wool skirt and black pumps. Black eyes. White face, smooth. It's like she's a chessboard come to life. She might be thirty-five.

At times she squints into her tablet to refresh her talking points and sometimes to reply to something or someone. I numbly go with the flow. Everything she's saying is science fiction to me right now.

"So my ex may have kidnapped our son. He's this … Eris?"

"It is a theory being investigated."

"You're saying Don is *two* people at once?"

She doesn't flinch but absorbs my anger. It's her job to be understanding. There's nothing creepier than professionalized empathy, the caregiver instinct as customer service. It's everywhere these days.

The dog must sense my rising anxiety. Tina waddles over to me, after warily watching us from her wicker basket in the corner. She pants at my feet, her moist pug eyes bulging with canine concern or confusion. The psychologist shifts her body slightly toward me, her long legs now sideways to the dog, as if she needs a protective flank.

"The clinical term is dissociative identity disorder," she says as if quoting from deep academic memory. "It is characterized by at least two distinct, enduring identities that control a person's behaviour and potentially exist in isolation from one another."

"Dr. Jekyll and Mr. Hyde." This comes out with a lunatic giggle.

"This is the presentation in popular culture," she continues, prickly. "This is one of the most controversial psychiatric disorders, with no consensus regarding its diagnosis or treatment. There is no empirically supported definition that this disorder exists …"

"Well, what is his second identity doing? I know the first one well enough."

"The theory is he hates the other part of himself. Wants to destroy the game."

"Sounds batshit crazy to me."

"Tell me, you've never had two voices at war inside you?"

And on and on she continues.

I'm trying to decode her voice — the accent, diction, syntax. Trying to understand where this woman comes from, and what her insides are like. But she's so completely armoured in her corporate professionalism, in her clinician's jargon. I don't get a sense of place or cultural background or roots. Maybe I just can't read people the way I used to. Or maybe she's too opaque. But I do know the posture, because mine is similar, if less robotic — or at least I hope so. Spend the years I have fighting for credibility and you can turn yourself into somebody you don't recognize at times.

I reach down to pet the dog, then shoo her away with a tap-tap-tap to her plump little bum. And off she reluctantly goes, back to the wicker basket. She hasn't been the same since Tony left us. My son isn't here to play with her, to feed her more dog treats than are good for her. She sleeps next to Tony most nights, a brown bundle of love on the pillow. Yes, two brown heads above the comforter. Now when I get up to use the bathroom in the night, she's often sitting by the window, staring into the city at rest.

The psychologist takes another swipe, then turns her unblinking eyes fully on me, as if demanding a response. I'm supposed to ask a question. That seems to be the imperative. But I want her to work harder here before I slip into whatever logic of interaction that maps to her therapeutically correct decision tree. I wait for more.

She swipes again. "All this raises many questions, you will agree."

"And what does Don say to these allegations?"

She nests the tablet in her lap with a gentleness that borders on a caress, then she says, officiously, "We have not shared our theories with him, yet."

"Should I assume the police are involved?"

"Much will depend on scenarios for when your son is located. If he is located."

"Please," I interrupt, choking back something. "It's not a 'scenario.' We are talking about a boy — our son. And, yes, his father."

She tilts away a smidge while stroking back a mass of curls that has plopped down into her face. "I'm so sorry if I have offended you," she says stiffly.

It's my first glimpse into the human in her. We study each other for an awkward minute. I wonder what she sees in me. Denial? Insanity? Rage? Deception? Could she be thinking I'm involved in whatever this is? Something is dying in me. My son has been missing for too long. My ex is accused of taking him. Can't be. I'm the one who feels crazed, out-of-body dissociated, as if I'm on the ceiling, looking down at two women who don't share a language but are still trying to work their way toward a deal.

Behind her, a wall of windows, revealing that the late-morning sky has just done something. The light has gotten colder, causing the sheen on her hair to go flat. It's not as naturally vivacious as I first thought. It's clearly been coloured up. Whispers of grey. None of this girlish observation is relevant except it reminds me that no matter how hard we try to control how we're perceived, there are factors out of our control that reveal us to others in ways not to our liking. She's my age, at least.

"I want to understand these clues you mentioned," I say.

She smiles — condescendingly, I think. I can't let that stand.

"Look, I'm a scientist. I get data. Predictive analysis, in particular."

"I have offended you again. Sorry."

I detect a wobble in her confidence. "Do you mind me asking, how well do you know Don?"

"I have treated him for years. His video diary was, I'm afraid, my idea."

Of course, the digital version of the Rothko Chapel.

The physical building, a non-denominational chapel built in Houston by wealthy art patrons, is as famous with the art history crowd as the Sistine Chapel, every wall given over to large minimalist paintings of black in subtle variations, the work of the American painter Mark Rothko.

When Don was looking for a metaphor around which to build a digital archive for his video diary clips, he was drawn to the Rothko Chapel, I believe, because of his egocentric notion that he, like Rothko, was a man of mystical insight, and that chronicling his reflections on his life experience and his inner world required a kind of holy or sacred process or place.

I struggled with Rothko's paintings as I interpreted them, their celebration of nuanced darkness. What was Don doing? Giving shape to his inner blackness, presumably? I did find Don's digital implementation idea compelling, though, turning each of the paintings into a portal, or screen, on which video clips would play, once summoned by simple, AI-based voice commands. Of course, with a digital reproduction on a small screen, you lose the monumentality of the paintings that Rothko was apparently striving for in the chapel interior. It didn't bother Don in the least that he was exploiting an artist, maybe even violating something important about how Rothko wanted people to experience his work. Typical Don. He had read that Picasso once said, on the subject of where his creativity and inspiration came from, "Good artists borrow — great artists steal." Whatever Picasso meant, I'm sure he didn't have in mind entrepreneurs like Don, who would gleefully use that argument to justify plucking ideas and concepts from so many others in creating Greenhouse, and rarely, if ever, acknowledging or compensating them for it.

In any case, we had a peaceful day at the Rothko Chapel, as I recall. Hours of earnest silence. What a trip! After a month alternating between a romantic getaway and doing an environmental assessment for an oil company operating in the Gulf of Mexico, I came home resolved to get pregnant. And also never to take oil money again. Don came home to his inner blackness, I guess, although to this day I have no idea what stories he fed into his beloved video diary.

"Isn't a more likely theory that Don is being set up?" I say.

"This is also being investigated."

If this woman wanted my attention, wanted me to talk, she's succeeding.

"What do you believe?" I ask, going on the offensive.

"My personal views don't count, clinically speaking. I am part of a larger group that is building toward a more refined probability assessment."

The tablet-swiping again — but with a twist. She hands me the device, telling me, "He may provide the answer you're looking for, himself."

It's a clip of Don from his video diary, which they've hacked.

> I'm sick. Broken into parts that don't
> know each other. What holds me

together? I'm like two different people. Ten people! Was I born this way? It sickens me how I shift from one face to another. I wonder how others do it. Who is unified? Maybe it's the spirit that lives between the faces that is real. The face in motion, in transition, becoming something else. I want to be one again, to be unified. A man transparent, honestly available, pure in my dimensions and to everyone in the same way. But I live in pockets of quiet deception. In silos of contradiction. There is always a danger, in diversifying your identity, that you will forget who you are and do things you don't think you're capable of.

Jun

I remember when they demolished Ai Weiwei's studios in Beijing and Shanghai because he was so vocal and unrelenting in his criticisms of the Party. Never thought the same thing could happen to me. I'm a corporate leader, not an artist or activist. I'm loyal to the Party and the regime. I pay off the right Princelings and their retainers. I share the wealth here and everywhere. But, without warning, and with only a scribbled demolition order that provides no rationale other than my architects hadn't followed all planning regulations, the wrecking crew showed up today in Longjing and flattened my house.

I remember when they took Weiwei into custody and how they treated him. This information wasn't so easily available in China, but no problem to find elsewhere.

And now I'm the one blindfolded in a fetid interrogation room.

I can smell the sweat and stink of the guards around me. I listen to them breathe, fart, shuffle their feet. I sense their boredom. I ask the room if I am allowed to lie down on the cot I'm sitting on. No one replies but when I do try to lie down, I'm roughly yanked up into sitting again.

It's been hours since I was picked up and blindfolded, probably approaching dawn. I doze off but am slapped awake after how long I don't know.

A door creaks open and others briskly walk in.

Someone pulls up a chair next to me.

"Must I wear this blindfold, or can we talk like civilized men?"

I hear whispering, a mix of Chinese and English, but can't make out words yet. The English voice is American, youthful, where the pitch rises at the end of every sentence or phrase, a habit my daughter has annoyingly picked up at Yale.

"Bai Jun." The man near me is clearly Chinese. "Tax fraud is a serious crime against the state. So is moving assets out of China without permission."

I mention a Politburo member I've long paid for protection. And then I'm slapped.

Now I hear the American, whispering or coaching my interrogator. Can't make out the words yet. Everything is silent for a long minute. Only the sound of a phone text being typed, the tap-tap-tap of a simulated typewriter.

"Your daughter," the Chinese interrogator says.

"Have you done something to my daughter? My wife?"

"Your wife! Let me explain the situation this way. We Chinese are quite capable of suppressing dissent when and where we need to. But so far, it's proven impossible to get past the doorman of your wife's building in Manhattan."

Laughter around the room.

"Your daughter," he continues. "That is a different matter."

"She is on American soil."

Then the American speaks up, in Chinese. "We have all the co-operation we need to bring her to China. She is in violation of several aspects of her visa. She can be charged with multiple crimes, given the assets in her name. She can be charged alongside you. A father-daughter reunion."

Slapped!

These shakedowns are usually conducted in a civil manner toward a clear objective so that company shares can change hands, or vineyards in France, or Vietnamese manufacturing plants, or even mistresses in London or Toronto.

"You know why you're here," my Chinese interrogator repeats.

"Please be specific."

"Your Security team is not being co-operative. You have an expectation that they will be able to uncover and disarm the cyber-actors now in the game. This is, we believe, beyond what they are capable of."

"If we allow the Pudong group into the game, there is every chance this situation will worsen with the Americans. We're talking about the cyberwarfare unit of the Chinese military. Our business could be destroyed. Shut down."

"Never mind the Americans. Our channel with them is open."

The rebuttal isn't fully out of my mouth when I'm slapped again. This time very hard. So I pivot as best I can. "What guarantees do I have that you will not destroy our business? Destroy the game to get what or who you're searching for?"

"There are no guarantees," says the American in Chinese.

The Chinese interrogator leans close to my face. Breathes at me. As he hovers over me, I try to brace myself for the next assault. But nothing comes. Nothing continues until I can barely breathe but I cannot let my guard down. I remain vigilant until I feel I will pass out. Nothing continues. It's a different kind of torture. The fear in waiting, not knowing, where anticipation ultimately becomes worse than the thing itself.

"You are aware Don Barton's son is involved," the Chinese interrogator says. "And possibly the father."

"This is an early Security assessment. I have trouble with the theory that Don Barton is involved. It seems implausible. As for the son, yes. A child. But I've given Barton my word I'll do everything I can to find his son."

The Chinese interrogator clears his throat, then. "Bai Jun, you have suffered greatly in your life. This is not a secret. Your parents. An unfortunate mishap during an unfortunate time for many families. But there will be a price to pay as the different actors in this situation assert themselves. You were orphaned at twelve or thirteen, and survived. Why not have confidence that a boy of fifteen can do the same?"

"I will give my approval for Pudong to access our core systems."

"That is a start."

"A start?"

Eris

I watch the action from the footage generated by our three drones that form the substance of the livestream link we made available on the big social platforms.

They're all up on the CN Tower in Toronto, on the platform below the telecom needle. A hundred storeys in the sky. Our two martyrs are standing beside the three Pornhome executives they've harnessed to the edge of the roofline. Two men, one woman, all in white jumpsuits. I preferred the original plan: castrating the men and decapitating the woman. But I didn't object to the final revisions to the creative strategy, because I'm not the one having to execute or die for it.

I see the black field of night framing their jumpsuit whiteness.

I can sense, feel, anticipate the blackness bleeding into white.

The wailing, the begging.

They recite scripts given to them by our martyrs, detailing their crimes of infecting the culture with viral strains of media disease. The script is aligned to the talking points in our brand strategy. And yet, there's hope in their voices that a confession will save them. But the harnesses are severed one at a time and, also one at a time, they fall screaming through the night to their black destiny below.

Silence for a moment beyond interpretation.

Then our two martyrs, talking to our drones, each in turn speak their last words to loved ones and to the world. Heartbreaking. Then they fall into the night.

Five people gone to their deaths. Three media criminals. Two martyrs. A flawless operation. Worldwide coverage, too.

For a long minute — more like two minutes — I mumble a wordless prayer to myself, communing with what or who I don't know, begging for forgiveness.

Now I instruct the Greenhouse team in the game to use my avatar to facilitate Tony through his next mission that, hopefully, will culminate with the hack of his father's video diary archive. I want him to see what his father is made of. Ordinarily, this would be an operation where I'd like to voice my own avatar. But over time, the team has gotten my linguistic response patterns down cold. Sometimes, as I monitor them in conflict-dialogue scenarios, it's eerie how they become me. A smarter me, too. While I am linked real time to all Eris dialogue in the game, I know that my time is best used thinking through next steps and letting our people interact with Tony.

With all that done, I step out from the guest house into tropical humidity and the lushness of things I will never learn to name. Small waves lap into white sand that's as finely grained as industrial salt, searing on the soles.

Here I am in the real world, which feels less real to me right now, with much less on the line — like the death of five people now on my conscience.

This small island, no bigger than a football field although well protected from storms by the headland of a larger island that curves around it, is technically controlled by the Belize government. In practice, however, as in many Caribbean island nations, this country is mainly controlled by offshore corporate money — some of it mine. There isn't much here, maybe a half-dozen structures scattered in the foliage behind the coastline. It's what you'd expect from a plutocrat keen on security and comfort but not ostentation that could attract pirates, local gangsters, or the global tax authorities — notably, the IRS.

I'm exhausted, legs trembling, ears ringing. My period is due but it's not going to come, yet again. Ever. The journey was difficult. Two days of problems. The plane needed its landing gear manually released after the avionics glitch. There were too many questions at border control in Belize about our passports that, to the agents, looked too new. And then there was my seasickness getting over to the island. On the sail over here, my Security team said it was necessary that I stay below the deck of the fishing boat, where the diesel fumes were unrelievedly heavy.

But here I am. And there she is: Rosa.

Golden skin, golden curls, playing in the sand with a yellow plastic shovel nearly as long as she is. Just turned five. It's all I can do to keep standing.

Her mother, Clare, stands over her, facing the water before turning slowly toward me. Topless. A yin-yang tattoo winking at me from above her bikinied hips. She still has that tiny waist but now she's got a sassy heft to her bum and tits that have been enhanced since my departure, expertly so. Can't all be Pilates and yoga. Or human potential seminars morning, noon, and night. I don't know how, in this light and heat, her skin can be so white.

It's not quite a faceoff between us but despite her smile, as genuine as it is, she's not running over to hug me. She's plainly tentative, as she should be.

"You thought you'd seen the last of me," I say as we inch together.

"We didn't want you to leave, but we understood why."

"But you didn't expect to see me again."

She scrunches her pretty face and starts to bow toward me — but catches herself. She knows I don't buy her fake submissiveness, a tic that doubtless developed in her deeply conservative upbringing in a hardcore Christian family, the daughter of Korean immigrants who ran a convenience store in suburban L.A.

In my peripheral vision on both sides of the beach — armed men.

There's no way anyone's leaving me alone with the little girl.

Clare reaches for her hand and together they gingerly walk toward me. Rosa's eyes are behind mirrored sunglasses with candy-bright orange frames.

My eyes.

Don

As I roam the game for hours at a time, I keep telling myself that there must be something I've missed, a clue.

My Toronto studio is a loft in the building where, years ago, we took Greenhouse global. The building is still owned by the company. It's wired with the network connections required for the integrated gaming environment that Greenhouse staffers installed yesterday while I stayed with Lily at her condo.

Lily thinks it pathetic that the better aspects of my character manifest in a simulacrum, a fake world. But how fake is it? At any given time, millions of members are active in the game, projecting their hopes and dreams, their fears and pathologies, too. It's a real community within its limitations. That it exists in a global cloud of servers and high-speed connections and is experienced on screens — is this only a bad thing? What I do know is that the game defines me as a man in all my turbulent fogginess, as a vessel for good and for bad, too, and for many things beyond that simplistic dichotomy. Things I don't or may never understand about myself.

Today's journey into the game is informed by a close reading of T-Redeem's data statistics, going back months. I decide to visit sectors where he's been active to see if there's anything I can learn before the hackers reappear, as they most certainly will.

I soar into the epic ruins of a car factory near Detroit, a composite sector of the game built up from stock images, especially of the old Packard Automotive Plant, which was something like the size of a hundred football fields. The world we created in this sector — not that many of our members would notice or even care — is less faithful to early-twentieth-century American brick industrial than perhaps it should be. It's too destroyed overall, the look and feel of Berlin at the end of the Second World War, mixed in with imagery appropriated from the Nazi camp aesthetic. Historical correctness lost out to the passion of one of my creative teams to relate environmental catastrophe to the Holocaust metaphor. I find the connection unconvincing, but our members love it.

T-Redeem's activity here had been focused on the long-term goal of landscape rehabilitation, which will take upward of twenty human years, or longer. The demolition work was started with a credit grant orchestrated by his hacker friends. Old factories are now being "eaten up" by characters designed to function as "site-specific locusts." Incredible to watch. The boy has several projects of this type going on. All require a massive allocation of member credits.

Next, I summon a game vista from our version of the Gulf Stream that separates Cuba from Florida. There's a war in progress here between the tuna hunters and those hunting the hunters, all funded by the hackers. I settle into an overhead viewpoint in the main conflict theatre. A part of me is thrilled to see what's happening. Tuna are being slaughtered in large numbers, but of course the schools just keep replenishing, unlike in the real world. To the untrained eye, it seems the tuna hunters are winning. The data tell me they kill tuna unchecked for hours and even days at a time, bringing them into Cuba and selling them for game credits to players in Tokyo, mainly. But now and then something beautiful happens, and so it does while I'm there: A tuna boat explodes from a missile fired from a submersible drone, a weapon system that takes a lot of credits to build and operate. The deeper I look into the boy's account, the more confused and opaque it gets. For months, credits were being funnelled to him through an impossibly complex nexus of transactions and anonymous funders. These hackers are incredibly smart. It appears to me they funded the Gulf Stream conflict simply to prove that our network administrators and gamemasters can't stop them from doing it.

What is their agenda beyond toying with the game?

I can't resist one more voyeuristic evaluation in a sector where the boy has lately been more than an incidental presence. It's our take on the Chernobyl nuclear disaster and the nearby city that was ruined as a consequence, Pripyat, now a ghost town, which we've rebranded Alienyet. Of course, we're not the first gaming conglomerate to create a Chernobyl-themed game, but we have the most complete offering. There's a war world for first-person shooters. A range of linear and non-linear storyline variables. We built in the obvious features, like the altered physics in certain areas that produce radiation, which can be deadly for players, killing them instantly or slowly, depending on the exposure time. Unlike other games in this category, we focus on game incentives to repair or reclaim the environment. But where our game really differs is connecting the local to the global, enabling action in Alienyet to affect events in other segments and vice versa. This is where the boy's genius shines. He and his associates have kidnapped environmental criminals from different sectors of the game and let them loose, unprotected, in the radiation zones, joined together in some type of chain gang, all slated to die horrible game deaths.

Again, they're out to prove that they, not our gamemasters, are in charge here.

Suddenly, a hacker avatar appears before me. Glowing and pulsating.

Meanwhile, the game backdrop evaporates. I'm now suspended in heavy liquid emptiness. I'm powerful as a gamemaster. It's going to take a lot of hacker muscle to harm me. But I activate my security halo anyway:

GM001: Where is my son?

Eris: You don't have a son now.

GM001: Please, no.

Eris: [no response]

GM001: Where is he?

Eris: He is Eris now.

GM001: He's a boy.

Eris: You will pay soon enough.

GM001: What do you want from him?

Eris: From him, nothing. From you, everything.

GM001: Let's hear it. What do you want?

An alert comes in with a non-standard beep. It's Eris. Wants to cut a deal. All right. Money. A hundred million in U.S.-denominated funds.

Tony

Up here in the attic of the farmhouse, it's impossible to tell what the weather outside is like. The windows don't open, for one thing.

Eris tells me the ankle monitor is supposed to protect me in case the government or my dad's security dudes break in to kidnap me. But that's bullshit. If they find me, what can she or her people do about it? Nothing.

T-Redeem: You can't do shit.
Eris: We will at least know if they take you.
T-Redeem: It's not like this will blow my leg off, right?
Eris: [no response]

I told Eris I've stopped taking the drugged-up juices. I play better without them, I think. But I'm sure I'm still being fucked with, drug-wise. Is there stuff in the microwaved meals? Who knows? I do know there's a smell that comes into the room through the heating and AC vents. I'm pretty sure they're misting me with something.

When I got here, she warned me not to go out at all, in case I'm seen.

Fuck it.

I step outside, into the field, but within minutes, two big dudes on an ATV come at me from the woods and hustle me back into the farmhouse. After they leave, I ping Eris through the headset.

Eris: They are on our team to protect you, us.
T-Redeem: They fucking grabbed me.
Eris: You were resisting.
T-Redeem: Getting tired of this.
Eris: Please, T-Redeem.
T-Redeem: I can't take this.
Eris: We're almost ready for the next mission.

After we disconnect, I heat up and eat my lunch. Soon I'm fighting the urge to sleep. Definitely drugs in the food. What can I do? Stop eating?

I go up to the attic and lie down next to the window.

I have views to the pond and beyond that to a marsh and beyond that a forest.

Suddenly, a deer appears in the clearing, followed by two fawns. Gotta be a momma deer. All three, golden. They look so innocent.

Until the shot rings out, and momma goes down. The babies scatter.

The same dudes on the ATV come out of the trees and haul away the dead deer. I sit there and watch, trying to stay awake.

In the pond, ducks are roaming around in some kind of duck armada. There's a seriously intense-looking bald eagle, wow, atop the beaver hutch at the pond edge, indifferent to two airborne crows duelling for hunting territory with a hawk.

I try to imagine the scurrying in the marsh by the mice and other small critters fearing that they'll end up as bird or coyote food.

Oh, I'm fading—

When I awaken, hours later, the sun is nearly down and the clouds have rolled in from wherever the fuck clouds come from, the golden landscape going brown, and the blue of the pond going grey.

It's peacefully beautiful, so still.

I'm thinking of that momma deer and her babies. How come I don't feel much? How come the tears don't come? How come?

I've killed so many characters inside the game. Tortured, abused, fucked with them. That's the game. The joy of it. And what about sadness?

I want to feel more than I do.

> Eris: Ready?

No time for doubts as we enter the game again on another mission.

We're in this super-huge parking lot, or something that looks like one. A square, that's the word. Surrounding the space on all sides are these Greek-looking temples.

Each building is guarded by hundreds of Protectors, rendered as usual with the complete absence of facial features: no eyes, nose, mouth, nothing. The theatre is bright from overhead suns. At least four suns.

We hover in the empty square.

T-Redeem: Where are we?

Eris: Greenhouse corporate HQ, the virtual home.

T-Redeem: I am by myself. Where are you?

Eris: You are alone but I am with you.

T-Redeem: Where?

Eris: Inside your point of view?

T-Redeem: Why aren't they attacking us?

Eris: We have negotiated with your father.

T-Redeem: What?

Eris: Matters related to compensation.

T-Redeem: Like how much we get paid to not mess the game up.

Eris: Precisely.

T-Redeem: You said nothing about needing money from my dad.

Eris: It's all part of our important work.

GM001: Son, just do what she says for now.

My father is talking to me on a public channel. He probably knows that Eris is taking up space next to me on this mission.

First, we do a tour of the square. We float past the teams of Protectors gathered in front of the buildings. I know that one Protector working behind the scenes, physically based in the support centre, equals like a hundred characters in the game. Either way, there's a serious Security team on alert. Maybe a hundred real people somewhere. Protectors are fun to mess with. They deploy in sectors as both good and bad characters, all depending on the number of members in play. Their basic job is to keep the fighting going. So it's a little weird to see them all standing at attention, doing nothing. I feel like blowing them away, severing all their heads for fun.

Up ahead, one of the temples turns gold.

GM001: Your money's in there. All of it.
Eris: Oh, this is a decimal point of your revenue stream, nothing more.

A transaction portal opens up and we slide into the gold temple.

In seconds, Eris's avatar turns gold.

Eris: The ransom, as agreed, well received.
GM001: Now our son comes back to us safe.
Eris: That is the arrangement.
GM001: Where is his actual GPS location?
Eris: Once we are done.
GM001: That wasn't our deal.
Eris: Our deal has other elements we still need to talk about.
GM001: If he is harmed ...
Eris: Say no more.

Just as we exit the temple, the Protectors line up along the flight path for us to reach a departure portal. My father's avatar hovers with us.

Suddenly, we veer away to a corner where two buildings pull apart enough for us to squeeze through — then smash shut, leaving my dad outside.

GM001: You have no clearance in that zone.

Eris: We have work to do.

GM001: What?

Eris: We are showing Tony who you are, your chapel experience.

GM001: He's just a boy.

Eris: In forty-eight hours, we will be in touch.

GM001: This is not what we agreed to.

Eris: If you want to see him alive, you will agree to this.

Eris shuts down all comm channels, in or out.

We're on our own now in a theatre that presents another game landscape I've never seen before. It's the quietest place, like the countryside: open fields, a forest here and there, ravines, rivers. In the game, the countryside is always dangerous. There's always an enemy waiting to surface out of something that looks innocent.

We're really moving fast over game terrain, faster than I'm ever able to go myself. Eris's character values have taken over. I don't know where she is, but wherever that is, I'm in the game through her point of view. We're racing toward a building on the horizon. It looks like Eris wants to crash it, but we pull up into top-down aerial. It's a steel-coloured place with eight sides, a low-rise structure, the roof frosted like ice, one big skylight. It sits on a cliff overlooking the ocean. I take a quick look at the vitals. This is stuff we don't see in the game. The ocean isn't a regular game-designed ocean. It has other properties in the data profile that I don't understand.

Eris: Eight sides — the octagon — you know what that is?

T-Redeem: It's how those ultimate fighting cages are built.

Eris: An octagon is often found in structures for contemplation.

T-Redeem: Sorry? What?

Eris: Churches, temples, chapels, you know.

T-Redeem: My father built something like that?

Eris: Yes, a church to all he has done, to all he needs to atone for.

T-Redeem: Atone means what?

Eris sweeps us down into this church or whatever it is through the skylight, which isn't virtualized glass but a gas, or cloud, covering the open space inside this octagon thing. And once inside, Eris gives us a slow room-spin. There's little here other than huge wall screens, one for each of the eight walls.

T-Redeem: Do we blow this shit up?

Eris: No.

T-Redeem: Then what?

Eris: Inside these screens are stories, confessions. Your father's diary.

T-Redeem: I'll be fucked.

Lily

I get a message from Don. Says he's been in contact with the hackers. Says Tony is alive — rather, his game avatar says he is. Which isn't the same, of course, as seeing him in the flesh. Don wants me to come down to the studio later tonight. He has a meeting first with Bai Jun to discuss the situation.

My God! Maybe there's hope after all!

Can I trust Don right now? If he wants payback, as he once warned, I had better not go down there alone. I call the corporate psychologist — or whatever she is — who arranges for a car to meet us downstairs in an hour. She will accompany me, along with Security.

At the appointed time, I climb into a black SUV driven by an over-muscled man, also in black, a cable corkscrewing out of his ear. As we drive toward the lake, the psychologist keeps stating numbers across the luxurious gloom of the rear seat, trying to draw my attention to her data, the digital trail that has led some to hypothesize that Don is at least two people in one body. She's delusional if she thinks I'll accept a bunch of spreadsheets flashed at me without a chance to deconstruct her work. She's about as real to me now as a character in a game, a series of orchestrated gestures that don't add up to a complete human. What else did I expect? Was he fucking her, too? She comes out of my husband's dreams, his domain of the digital make-believe, where I not only lost him, or we lost each other, and lost our child. Our Tony.

She is relentless. And totally blind to social cues. It seems I need to be enlightened non-stop by her command of digital analytics. I ask her to stop several times. And then, finally, I reach over and clasp her chin in my hand — not her throat, not that yet — and say nothing more. And only then does she retreat in vivid comprehension.

Sometimes the only thing that's real in this blasted world is the physical: the reality and the consequence of human touch. The violence of touch, too.

The journey ends near the marina, down by the docks. It's the first time I've been here in years. There's a mothballed power plant nearby, and along the canal are raw materials piled up in towering pyramids that have arrived or are about to go out on tankers. When Don's business started to expand, they bought a five-storey cinder-block building here where they staffed up what amounted to a giant frat house. We mortgaged everything to finance it. I said don't buy it. The building was on poisonous ground where a smelting operation had once been. No one cared about that. It was cheap space.

As we turn into the driveway, I tell my companion that, on second thought, it's best if I go in there alone. And if I need help, she'll be the first to know. My sense is if I show up with a psychologist, Don will have his guard up and that must be avoided right now.

Could he be that sick? If so, who would he be trying to hurt? It would have to be me. Could he really be out for revenge? Could he really be consumed by self-hate?

Jun

I am at the podium of a penthouse conference room in midtown Manhattan for our investor presentations. It's the usual group of analysts from the big firms and the boutiques. We just released our quarterly results this morning. Another record quarter. Revenues and earnings are way up. In any other situation, these results would send the stock soaring. That's not what's happening today. Rumours of hackers loose in Greenhouse have come out of Hong Kong and several Eastern European countries, causing a steady decline in the stock. That's all the analysts assembled today want to talk about, not our record quarterly results.

One says, "What can you tell us about this hack? The game is working as usual."

"We can't be certain if it is hackers or just a changing pattern in the game activity."

Another says, "You lost a hundred thousand members. That's what the blogs say."

"User attrition isn't unusually high against our total customer base."

My, how petulant they all look — childlike. The questions come one after another and my answers, which are evasive but not criminally so, come one after another until everyone tires from the lack of true and plain disclosure. I've done my job well and now I need to get to the airport and fly to Toronto to meet with Don. For the first time in I don't know how long, I'm heading into an important meeting unclear of my motivations and objectives. Balancing my respect for Don as a treasured colleague with my fiduciary responsibility as Greenhouse CEO will be difficult. There's also the matter of the safety of myself and my daughter. What I do know is that I'm paid to manage these difficulties. Whether I do so successfully is an open question.

When the meeting breaks up, our PR people lead me into the penthouse lobby where the analysts are buzzing around the buffet tables. There's a protocol at these meetings to engage in informal chit-chat afterward, but I've instructed my PR people to march me through the buffet toward the elevators. But as the doors close, I'm all alone with one of the young analysts, and no PR guard to protect me. His ID badge says he's associated with a hedge fund with offices in the British Virgin Islands and the Channel Islands. And now he's got me alone. I will have to fire our local team for this.

As we start to descend, I notice that he's smiling at me. I grimace back.

"Bai Jun, your answers were perfect," he says in Chinese. I recognize the voice from the interrogation room in China — the American. He knows I've picked up on who he is.

"It is best that I don't ask which investors you represent," I say. "It is also best I don't ask how you ended up alone in this elevator with me."

"Thank you for facilitating the board's agreement to negotiate with the hacking group so that they don't do something … apocalyptic."

"It was an expensive gesture. Depleted our cash reserves. But done."

"The money will be put to good use."

"Excuse me — how would you know that?"

"We've infiltrated one of their cells. That's all you need to know right now. At some point, we'll get the funds back. There are better uses for it, I can assure you."

"We?"

"Consider the ransom the price for not being investigated for corruption."

"Permit me one question for you and your associates."

"We have ten floors to go."

"What is more important to you: Stealing money by blackmailing legitimate businesses, or stopping a global security threat? It is hard to know whether you're just a criminal gang or working in the best interests of the countries involved. Or both?"

"Sometimes in our trade, we exploit economic opportunities in one area that help us fund certain special operations in other areas that cannot be officially funded any other way. It is not an unusual approach. Decades ago, as I'm sure you know, in the Reagan administration, the intelligence operatives secretly sold arms, illegally, to Iran to pay for a dirty little war in Nicaragua."

"An enterprise that did not end well."

"With one question, you should have asked me why I'm here. You can't believe I'm here simply to thank you."

"We have five floors to go, still. Tell me."

"I'm here to inform you that not only do we have systems access, but our Security team has fully replaced yours. This is in the interests of national security for China and America. Also, the days of Greenhouse as a public company will come to an end very shortly with an offer that shareholders will not be able to refuse, especially a majority shareholder like your fund. You will also shortly be replaced as CEO and removed from the board. However, this is information you cannot share with Barton right now."

"And if I ignore this instruction?"

"We wish no harm to come to your daughter."

"I understand."

"We do, however, want you to speak to Barton. To see if he's learned anything that you will, out of the goodness of your heart, share with us."

"And if I ignore this instruction?"

"I don't like to repeat myself."

Eris

I'm sitting with Clare and Rosa under the beach umbrella when a male voice from behind disturbs the air. "Clare, call off the guards, please."

I look behind me to see Ray coming down the beach.

Clare does something on her phone. The guards disappear into the dunes.

Rosa is entangled in Clare's legs, only an arm's length away. So far, I've resisted the urge to reach for her. It's a privilege I've walked away from.

"You look like shit, honey," he says, embracing me as he sits down on a fluffy towel next to me.

So strong, yet so supple. I'm nearly undone by the earthy aroma of shea butter on his skin and in his hair. It triggers memories of his sweat on my skin when we made love. Clare didn't like the shea butter. But still, when they made love, as a duo, I felt their connection was the deeper one, even if my ovaries and womb delivered our child, not hers. Ray said he loved watching me and Clare together, but surely he knew we were mainly performing for him. There was, at times, an enjoyably superficial enthusiasm between Clare and me. But I never felt more disconnected from my body or desires than when I identified as polyamorous. I felt like the theory of the moment turned to flesh. Even now I'm not sure what I was doing, other than consciously rejecting convention.

When I gave birth to Rosa, however, I started to see our relationship through the lens of that ungainly term *throuple.* I had to: Real commitments were required. Domestic reality, not bliss, had arrived.

"I know this is not what we agreed to," I say to him, apologetically.

"It's definitely a risk," Ray says. But he's happy to see me.

Rosa kneels in the middle of the adult trio, her sunglasses in hand now, impishly staring at me but giving me the silent treatment. I wonder if she remembers me at all. Ray and Clare said one day she will be told more.

"So, no interest from the authorities, three years later," I say, and instantly regret bringing business into the moment. I'm otherwise lost for words.

"We're covered on the sale," Clare says dismissively, referring to the crypto exchange the three of us started and then sold to a global financial institution, the proceeds being the source of their wealth and what's left of mine. "Remember, the deal was papered in best practices. All by the book. Your work, mainly. And mine, a little. We've had the banks' lawyers poking around like hyenas. But there's nothing to find. It was clearly codified to the nines that it was buyer beware."

"But when you sell at the top before a market crash, someone will come after you," Ray says. "We'll see what the future brings. The hyenas will be back."

"Sounds good." I feel like an idiot. I didn't come here to talk money.

We sit there for an awkward moment until Rosa leaps up and starts running to the water, giving Clare an excuse to go after her.

I sit quietly with Ray, my gaze telling him I'm amused at yet another one of his transformations. When I first met him, he hadn't fully emerged from his academic persona, still partial to bespoke suits, colourful bow ties, and ornate syntax that together, it seemed to me, spoke loudly to his advanced Ivy League degrees in philosophy. But when we started looking for funding for our crypto start-up, he quickly morphed into a street-smart hustler, a rougher character who displayed mannerisms that he had obviously learned fighting his way out of a very poor, often violent Houston neighbourhood. And now? He's evidently gone all Bob Marley, or more generally Rastafarian, the dreadlocks flowing to his shoulders.

"I like the look, but if you're gonna appropriate, in this case you might consider hiding the Apple Watch on each wrist."

"You think I'm just a series of gestures, an empty suit," he says glumly.

"Not empty — just with an impressive wardrobe."

"My outside reflects my inside, I can assure you. And you?"

"I don't know, Ray. I struggle. There are moments when I know myself."

"Who you are … whoever it is … belongs here, Joanna."

"Please, don't."

"I still don't understand."

"Ray," I say, "as a child I felt a presence around my body, a bubble. The energy field of myself, flowing from inside out. Then suddenly it was gone. And it has never come back. Did you ever feel that way? I'm sure you did."

"Leaving aside the view that childhood memories are unreliable products of cognition," he says, "I'm curious where this is leading. Is this just a new way to criticize what we're doing, building a new life while you go off on your jihad or whatever it is?" This rebuke comes with a wink, telling me not to be offended.

"No, I just wonder what happened to me. How all that energy, how all that native intuition died out, got channelled into what made me, what defined me."

"Joanna, I've heard that rant how many times? How the media ecosystem, virtualization, whatever, stole your energy." He says this gulping out the words, impatient with me. "We're doing everything we can to raise our daughter away from the bullshit you're out there fighting to destroy."

What am I doing right now? God, I'm so vengeful. I'm trying to make them pay something of the cost I'm about to incur. Selfishly, I've walked back into their lives, it seems, for the purpose of ripping off the scab over the gash of our failed relationship.

I reach for his hand, and he takes it.

Rosa is hippity-hop running down the beach, Clare following her.

"It's my turn, if you'll allow me a little rant before you go," he says.

"I'll be gone as soon as the sun goes down. You have my word."

"Joanna, we both know that the story of rebellion or revolution offers as many cautionary tales as it does successes. One can fall in love, as I did, with the more inspiring forms of it. Say, non-violence combined with civil disobedience, and, yes, great personal sacrifice. MLK, right? But for every airbrushed fable of the Boston Tea Party or Mao's Long March, or the victories, small as they were, with the Civil Rights movement, we've seen so much chaos, extremism, terrorism, organized fanaticism. Everywhere on the planet. Is that really what you're about now?"

"I don't have a sound bite for you."

"Why must you tear everything down? Why only anarchy? Why not just step outside that and live in a better, parallel world, with us? Build your own reality."

"Parallel realities are a big part of the problem."

"Ah, I knew you'd come around to attacking us again."

"Oh, Ray. I'm so sorry. I shouldn't have come."

"Joanna, you really are going to die." Now tears fill his eyes.

There's nothing left to say or do. I get up, hug him, kissing away the tears that stream down his face. Then I stumble back to the guest house.

I patch into the Greenhouse team to deal with an alert escalation:

GH1: We're getting probes around the Greenhouse team?

Eris: What kind?

GH1: Some social engineering. A honey-trapper in Singapore.

Eris: Doing what?

GH1: Trying to fuck one of our top techs there. Same in Estonia.

Eris: And?

GH1: Nearly caught one with his pants down. But he knew it was fishy.

Eris: Anything else?

GH1: There are people knocking into but not through our backdoor tech.

Eris: Where's it originating?

GH1: Greater Chicago. But that could be a front, too.

Eris: We have operatives there. Worked the CN Tower action.

GH1: You mean the guys who came to us from the Chinese dudes?

Eris: Yes.

GH1: The Chinese dudes were all killed, trying to blow up the Apple plant.

Eris: But they were above board. Weren't they?

GH1: I don't fucking know anymore. Felt like it.

Eris: Can you tighten the security protocols?

GH1: We have. But there'll come a point when all hell breaks loose.

Eris: How so?

GH1: As we get deeper into the game platform, there's more on the line.

Eris: Explain "line" to me.

GH1: With hooks into fifty fucking million members, think of the damage!

After I patch out, I realize that an afternoon shower is over us, the rain drumming softly on the metal roof. The kind of sound that puts you to sleep. So I try. The more rest the better before the long trip back. But sleep is denied. Too much to think about. I find myself going over the past in search of justifications:

I picture my therapist the day he came to the youth psych ward all those years ago. He settled across from me in the common room. A blunt but caring man.

I picture my hands, nails bitten down, my skin blotchy pale.

I feel the stitches over my right eye where someone had ripped out the piercing before my father found me, overdosing in the alley.

I hear the labels that had been thrown at me since I was a teenager. Antisocial disorder. Borderline. Attention-deficit hyperactive. Clinical depression.

"Well, here we are again," he said. "Another fucking date with destiny."

"I need a smoke."

"The last time they let you out for a smoke with the orderly, you took off, bare feet, no coat, and got into a taxi and paid with cash. How you managed to do this, I have no idea. But it's impressive."

"They can't hold me forever."

"No, you'll be out by the weekend. Perhaps dead by Monday night."

"I just want a smoke."

"There are ways we can arrange that," said my therapist.

I remember feeling that it took everything within him to feel any compassion for me, as opposed to pity or anger. I later learned that the week before he had lost two of his clients, both teens, both overdosed.

That day in the psych ward, with cordial indifference, I told him more.

Being on my stomach, surfing the carpet, sniffing for grains of cocaine.

On the phone, after a week without a shower or brushing my teeth, begging my parents for money.

At the pawnshop, shakily handing over the watch, the only cherished possession my father still had from his father.

I picture my therapist reaching into his coat and pulling out an envelope.

"Your itinerary to Miami."

"I'm not going into treatment."

"Sweetie, I'm fucking tired of funerals. So understand something. Your parents love you. But, at this rate, you are going to die. And as painful as this will be on your mother and father, they will survive your death. Do you understand?"

Eventually, I did understand.

My parents, bless their corporatized ignorance, could not accept my rejection of the blue blazer and tartan miniskirt of the girls' school where my mom had once been head girl. And yet, over time, I became a version of them. Didn't I? In eras past I would have been trundled off to a nunnery or monastery for the problems I caused as a teenager. Or burned at the stake or broken on the wheel.

For years the meds clouded everything about me until I took control of my body. History will not be kind to the corporate scientists and propagandists behind early-generation selective serotonin reuptake inhibitors given to children and teenagers. In the future, we will look at SSRI theory much like we now look at cocaine or lobotomies, which were both known as wonder treatments in a previous era.

What kind of mother am I?

What kind of person will my daughter become after I die?

Don

Everything's happening so quickly.

I don't want to leave the studio after the stunt Eris pulled, diverting Tony into my video diary following the ransom transaction. Still, Bai Jun insists on meeting after his plane lands in Toronto, before he heads back to China. Says it's important and related to Tony's situation. I tell him he can have thirty minutes, then I need to get back, as Lily will be arriving. I also need to get back in the game, regardless of what Eris said. They've fucked with the deal. So will I.

Bai Jun is alone when I enter the private dining room on the top floor of the museum. It's a cavernous attic, the interior strictly obedient to the explosive angles of the roof, an enclosure of fractured volumes that intersect in service to a design that apparently simulates the experience of being inside a crystal. I don't care how many steel beams went into bolting this place together, I don't feel psychologically at ease here. You feel something's about to fall on you at any moment.

He comes forward to hug me. "It is difficult to say what our strategy should be," he says, massaging my shoulder with one hand, handshaking with the other. "But your boy will come home safe. We must believe this."

The dining room is empty except for us. There's only bottled water and two glasses on a small table between two chairs. No evidence we'll be eating. Bai Jun isn't in North America exclusively for me. He's been in New York this week, talking up the company to investors about our financial results and, disturbingly, the recent fall in the stock price.

"Bai Jun, how can you be so confident?"

"I have never betrayed my commitments to you. I have always introduced orchestrated speed into our responses."

I respect his non-idiomatic way with English — so precise.

A capable man: All the right political credentials at home, an MBA from an important business school in France, followed by years on Wall Street, learning at the feet of serious hedge-fund guys. He was a saviour when we needed money to expand the Greenhouse business as it grew globally. Before anyone really knew it, his syndicate owned our company, fixed up our balance sheet, moved our design operation and headquarters to Hangzhou, and then rapidly replaced most of my executive team with Chinese nationals.

The merger wouldn't have happened unless the two of us had bonded. My three other co-founders and our bankers hated doing a deal with the Chinese. They found Bai Jun and his people to be unpredictable and persistently hypocritical as deal negotiators. Typical paranoid responses to the Chinese. I just thought they were creative. Our advisors preferred a deal with Disney or Microsoft. I didn't see it that way. Greenhouse's biggest growth market is Asia. We needed a Chinese or Korean partner, end of story. Anyway, I was the largest shareholder and made the call myself about whom to partner with. In retrospect, it's easy to see why my colleagues and our advisors didn't like Bai Jun or his people. They were just as wealthy and self-important as we were or wanted to be. He is a little like me: He came out of nowhere, hungry for something better. And there was some trauma in his life I could sort of identify with, although he suffered so much more. His parents were banished to the countryside during the Cultural Revolution. And executed. He has talked about owning nothing but a rucksack of clothes, moving from village to village at the whim of Party cadres.

"Bai Jun, we've always been honest with one another. All this seems rather excessive, meeting under these circumstances. What is going on that we could not discuss by other means?"

A plume of vape smoke rises upward, as he thinks this over. "The authorities. It is less the local level, although some police entities are now officially advised. Tony is classified as a runaway or missing person, but I do not understand Canadian law sufficiently to evaluate this. We are also in discussions now with national security and counterterrorism operatives."

"This is putting my son at risk."

"The discussions — which, I have to say, we initiated in some cases — have been done under secure tradecraft protocols."

"How can you be so sure the hackers won't learn of this?"

More plumes of vape smoke. He turns his back to me, not rudely, but to think for a minute. Exterior light and city views flood into the dining room through windows that gash into the sloping walls and ceilings in assertive parallelograms. These prismatic openings seem just the thing to set off migraines. The angular weirdness betrays a lack of confidence in the city. Toronto isn't being trusted to deliver an aesthetic wallop within rectangular frames of transparency. A bizarre space. It could be the departure lounge for a space-shuttle service. Or the courtroom in a sci-fi movie where fascist aliens with massive brains and soprano voices condemn the democracy-loving Earthlings to death.

I just stand there, expecting more from him.

"The hackers are now operating within the deepest game layers with your son, going through this video archive of yours," he continues. "We believe this could be a diversion, as other hackers from the group are operating in other sectors."

"Where is this leading?"

"There are intelligence operatives in China and in the U.S. who believe it is possible that a terrorist group may be using the game as a medium to execute an operation. The American government is being quite difficult now. They have not forgiven us for acquiring control of your company. They want our guarantee that cyberterrorism activity is not being generated or supported within our game. The discussions with the Americans and the Chinese government are extremely complicated. It is a kind of bureaucratic insanity. But others are watching us. What is it they say? If the right thing is not being done, it must at least be seen as being done. Everybody is watching everybody."

"You are not being clear enough with me."

He restrains a smile, turns it into a grimace. "To be honest, there will be reasons that will be natural for some authorities to investigate you."

"Natural reasons?"

He shakes his head. I'm being dense.

"Certain people will want to know precisely everything about your recent interactions with your son. When you last saw him in person. They will look to you to help define the direction of the investigation."

"I have nothing to hide, Bai Jun."

"I am saying we are operating within surveillance complexity."

"You're not telling me much."

He doesn't like my anger but maintains his composure: "I would like to be kept informed — for your safety, for our business, but mostly for the safety of your son."

"Informed of what?

"Of what you are learning about the hackers. What you are doing in the game to uncover them. We have paid a ransom, but still the situation is not resolved."

"My son's life is at stake."

"It is important to co-operate with them as much as possible."

He's being too diplomatic by half. I need to keep thinking here.

In the takeover process, he was always savagely direct. It was part of his charm. But that was then, and this is now. Perhaps I've yet to calibrate fully the implications of the changing power relationship between us. It's true that, being on indefinite sabbatical, I don't have an active role in the business, other than to mentor a few game designers whom his executives hired to create new products for our Asian markets. But it's also true that I still sit on the board of directors, the only Westerner there, the only co-founder of the predecessor company to survive the takeover. I'm a member of the executive committee of the board that evaluates his performance and determines his compensation. In a sense, as the CEO, Bai Jun must play politics with me.

If that's why he's being opaque with me, I don't like it.

"As I said, you're not telling me something."

He smiles, accepts graciously that I've insulted him in a way he can't possibly take offence to. It's my child in danger, not his.

"If you ever feel a need to confide in me, to tell me anything, any secret, it will be safe with me," he says. "We must trust one another."

I'm still not sure where he's leading me, but soon enough, he's gone. Puzzled by the encounter, I make my way downstairs and exit into an unseasonably balmy dusk. I'm feeling faint from lack of sleep. I'll get some air, then head back to the studio.

This is the wealthiest shopping district of the city. The high streets and all the cute Ye Olde Laneways celebrate retail brands of global consequence. The streets reveal a well-fed population in many skin colours. The skyline aspires to the futuristic and, if not quite as manically vertical as China's cities, it sprouts everywhere with building cranes. The city will never acquire the classic metropolitan grit — at least to my middle-aged eyes — of New York or Paris, or the reclaimed medieval weirdness of Bruges or Tallinn. It'll never romance me with a Renaissance past capable of launching a million art books. But Toronto is shedding its reputation as New York run by the Swiss. It's more like Singapore run by Starbucks: a youthfully hyper-caffeinated city, but not particularly sensually energized.

I was raised a dozen blocks from here, Regent Park, a difficult place in my youth, quite often violent. Until I started strength training in my late teens, I was a skinny thing, always the last one chosen for games of shinny or schoolyard baseball. At home I was incubated in an airless brick box of an apartment. The classic latchkey kid, the only child, my mother a barmaid, my father a roofer. I was sixteen when they died in a car crash. Once I got past the shock, I was at last free to run away, to imagine a future far different from one they could have pointed me toward. There was just enough insurance money to drop out and play with computers for two years. Strange, in the hundreds of hours I've devoted to my video diary, I haven't given much thought to what it means to be parentless at sixteen. It's hard to say whether it made me more or less sensitive to pain, to death, to loss. It seems I've spent a lifetime analyzing myself and changed nothing in the process, other than acquiring a perception of myself as a special case, as a unique specimen of insight and existential sensitivity.

What have I achieved with these meditations?

I vomit into the grass, until there's nothing left inside me.

Tony

T-Redeem: Aren't we kind of trapped in here?

Eris: They will not disturb us. Your father won't.

T-Redeem: I'm getting tired of hanging by myself. That wasn't the deal.

Eris: That time will soon come to an end ... but first you have homework.

T-Redeem: Fuck homework.

We're in this space, like a church or something, where all these screens are supposed to be portals into my dad's video diary. How it's organized, I have no idea. Eris seems to know. It's all voice recognition. You say a word, or a phrase, and the video thumbnails present. Eris's doing the work, summoning clips that go back years.

T-Redeem: What are you looking for?

Eris: Things your father is ashamed of.

T-Redeem: I don't get it.

Eris: It is the only place he has tried to tell the truth.

Video clips unfold, one after the other.

My father as a young man, against a white wall. He just looks goofy. When he starts to talk, it seems like he's acting, way too concerned there's an audience he's talking to. He tells the camera, stuttering, he wants to start over. The first clips don't say much. A lot of whining about work, about how hard it is, how tired he is all the time, how he can't seem to find the right ideas or something. One clip gets my attention as he goes on about a chat group where he had been talking with someone about creating a game that sounds like Greenhouse. A war game about the environment. In the clip he says it was a great idea, something to talk to the guys about at the lab.

Eris: Your father is a thief, his ideas not his own.

T-Redeem: Where does he say he stole something?

Eris: There's enough here to cast doubt.

The clips jump ahead in time, a few years. My father is older — calmer, too. It's around the time that Greenhouse was developed, when I was a baby. He goes on and on about how excited he is about the game, although in some of the clips he complains that he's spending no time at home with me and Mum, and the problems he's having with that. He starts to talk about some business shit I can't follow.

T-Redeem: What's the point?

Eris: It's about money — backdating stock options.

T-Redeem: Like insider trading, yeah, I've heard of that.

Eris: Something like that.

T-Redeem: Is it illegal, what my dad was doing?

Eris: He never says he's done anything, just thinking of doing it.

T-Redeem: Like casting doubt, as you said before.

Eris: You learn fast.

More clips.

I know most of this shit. Boring. My dad talking about how things went bad between him and Mum. So, like, my dad had like a girlfriend at work, or something like a girlfriend, who was causing him headaches, money. No, it's like three girlfriends. All at once. Also, shit, he admits to fucking Big Sister in a hotel room after Mum fired her. I'm jealous! A bunch of clips on that. My dad sounding guilty or sad. Then angry at Mum for being such a bitch to him. She often complained about Dad being away, but I didn't know she hated his work, found it disgusting what he was doing with Greenhouse.

T-Redeem: So my father and mother are not perfect. Are you?

Eris: What I am is not the issue.

T-Redeem: What are you going to do with this stuff?

Eris: We want you to understand why the game must be destroyed.

T-Redeem: Uh, I get it. Now what?

Eris: The game gets real, T-Redeem — but first one more clip.

T-Redeem: I'm tired of all this.
Eris: Don't you want to see what your father has done to you?

The clip is mostly like the others. Just my dad talking into his phone. And what I hear, while not that unexpected, is nothing any kid wants to hear from his father.

> Contrary to our purpose, what we've built, what I've dreamed up, really, is a vehicle for turning youthful curiosity and hormones into addiction, into individual and crowdsourced sickness. Pathology. I changed the world, yes, but how?

Lily

I don't want to go into this building again. On the top floor, he'll be itching behind his consoles, his face lit by screen glare, the sonic gulf between us filled with keyboard noises and game effects. The building was mostly abandoned after the business went to China. What a waste: All the money we spent on rewiring the place top to bottom. It's now a ghost of itself, inhabited by one ghostly figure who made it all happen, my ex, a man I need to assess quickly, which seems impossible, given that I was apparently unable to do so in our years together.

As expected, he's in his gaming uniform of black everything: the jeans, the T-shirt, the shoes. When he hears me approaching, he lifts his head for an instant, then turns back to his screens. He looks like hell. In an exhausted tone, he says, "Bai Jun seems to think I'm under investigation in Tony's disappearance."

"We have things to talk about."

He indicates that I look overhead: surveillance cameras, everywhere.

"They move as I move," he says. "I lead, they follow."

In the kitchen, while he prepares two cappuccinos, I tell him that his corporate psychologist said there's a theory out there that he might be involved in Tony's disappearance. He's either indifferent or stunned, I can't tell.

Calmly, too calmly, he says, "Whatever happened to client-patient confidentiality?"

He sounds like a sociopath to me.

"I'm no lawyer, but if there's a crime somewhere, a therapist has a responsibility to alert the authorities. Doesn't she?"

"Something very strange is going on."

"Are you this crazy person they think you might be?"

"Fuck no, but I'm not concerned about that. I am doing real work right now."

"I'm concerned about it, definitely."

He turns away from me. "I will co-operate with this witch hunt as long as they leave me alone here to do my work. They can watch me all they want. I have nothing to hide."

There's a clear and present desire to strike him across the face.

He looks at me until I stumble backward over a nest of cables, moving away until I bounce into the floor-to-glass windows offering views toward the city. I slide to the floor, causing a mini dust storm around me. I turn myself into a kind of tent, cross-legged, hunched forward, hands steepled over my face, hiding myself from everything in this room. When I look up, he is so calm — scary calm.

"There are reasons to be angry with me," he says. "But not because I've done anything to harm our boy. You don't believe I could harm him."

"I don't know what to believe."

He puts his hand out and I grasp it so that he can help me to my feet.

"Tell me why you are not this crazy person," I say, as he turns his back to me and walks toward his consoles.

"You will tell yourself soon enough."

He jumps into the cockpit of his console and starts to drum fingers on his lips, a gesture I've always found annoying, as if he's deciding how much of his twisted brilliance I can absorb at any given moment.

"Be absolutely clear with me."

"There are different players in the game now. Big forces. All watching me. Of course they know I made contact with the hackers and with Tony after I detected patterns in his older game activity in tunnels within the admin system — where he escapes detection and moves around."

"I can't follow all this. What is going on? Where is our son, Don?"

"After discussions I had with Bai Jun and the company board, they agreed to pay a ransom to release Tony. But then Eris pulled a fast one after we paid the money, locking our son in my video diary."

"Don, where is our son? His living body! You have to do better than that."

"He's safe for now. Or at least I was led to believe that. There's no way to know. The hackers sealed off the video diary. They might still be in there, of course, but we still don't know where they are, physically. Could be anywhere on the planet."

"Where the fuck is he?" This approaches a scream.

I'm tumbling over toward him, fighting through the cables, banging my hip into the edge of the console, staggering and reeling toward him. And he's braced, now, ready to receive me, stiff-armed, hands in front of him, as if to say, *Hold on, hold on a minute.*

"I don't know," he shouts at me. "I was told to wait. And wait we will."

Jun

My secure phone rings up an incoming call. The American.

He says, "You spoke to Don Barton. So the transcripts indicate. But your conversation, by the sounds of it, was … oblique. You learned very little."

"I thought it best to let him come to me, not to insist on disclosure. But to trust me. To trust our relationship. To come to me if he needs help."

"It is debatable whether you're acting in good faith here. It would have been helpful to learn more about his interactions with the hackers."

"If I had been any more direct with my questions, he would have smelled, how do you say it, a rat? Anyway, you can track his movements in the game."

"Not as well as we'd like. His gamemaster tools wipe clean his activity before we can study it. We've yet to solve this."

"I'm sorry I couldn't do more to help in this instance."

"You need to do better in future."

I'm finally victimized by my own anger. "Listen to me, just this once. We paid a significant ransom that will apparently end up with you and yours. You resolve this."

"Direct control over Barton we currently do not have."

My turn to threaten. "Do I need to speak to my friends in the Politburo?"

"This would be suicidal for your standing in China and deadly for your family."

"You may leave me no choice if your thuggish behaviour continues."

"Bai Jun, calm down. There is a strategy in place to remedy the situation. In due course, the ideological fanatics will be addressed with extreme prejudice."

"In due course, my friend, I will deal with you, regardless."

A spooky laugh, then. "So the real Bai Jun finally shows his colours. We know you've taken matters into your hands before. Violently so. I believe there are at least two former associates of yours at the bottom of Victoria Bay, encased in concrete."

Silence serves me better here.

I didn't think, years ago, that allowing that rumour to spread was in my best interests. But over time I've enjoyed the benefits of allowing a lie to become truth.

Eris

As my plane sweeps up through serene oceanic blue, banking northbound for the trip back, I'm reflecting, sad as I am, on the origins of my purpose. It's the only thing that will stop me from turning this plane around and going back to Rosa.

Uncannily, the story flows in three memories that live within me with cinematic fidelity.

First memory:

High above the Atlantic, I'm next to Don Barton on the company plane when the co-pilot comes into the cabin with two trays, each featuring a marbled slice of Wagyu beef on bone china and a glass of expensive red. He says that for dessert, we have a choice between a hazelnut torte or a buttery rhubarb crisp. All this from a greying, middle-aged man who wears a peaked hat crested with the corporate logo and a white short-sleeved shirt with gold-striped epaulettes.

"I'm not hungry right now," Don says. "What about you, Joanna?"

"Same." It's a career-limiting mistake to eat while your CEO doesn't.

"Care for a glass of red?"

"I don't drink."

I'm here as a fluke of executive whim to present the business case for the new Greenhouse billing architecture that my boss, and her boss, thought perfect for the next upgrade cycle. They wanted to take credit for the work. But Don wanted me, the girl in the trenches with the other finance nerds. He was good that way, capable of seeing through bureaucracy and recognizing the real contributors.

He's intriguing to look at and knows it. A wiry six-footer, partial to rimless glasses and oval lenses that signify cultivated brainpower and corporate arrogance. The rumour is that he invests in his appearance. Surgical work. The interventions, if they are there, aren't in service to an alien condition of youthfulness. I suspect he's tried to make himself look wiser. There's a scar along his jaw he apparently acquired in launching Greenhouse in Russia.

"I'll tell you why you're here," he says. These are his first words to me, an hour into the flight. "Because you know what we're trying to achieve."

"Mr. Barton, I feel that —"

"If you're on this plane, you've earned the right to call me Don."

"Okay."

"You understand how to sell *compulsion*."

"Sorry?"

"The billing model you're proposing is very clever," he says. "Almost maliciously so."

"No, it's based on the idea of responsible playing, helping gamers set limits, not spend beyond what they can afford. Providing help to those who get in debt. Putting restrictions in place for people who can't stop themselves."

"Of course that's the superficial intent. Or perhaps a conscious rationale. If you really thought about what you've designed, you would see something different at work under the marketing generalities. You'd see you were giving players the illusion of control for limiting their destructive play, but in fact, with all the tiering of incentives and the bonus levels, gamers will be exposed to a continuous dopamine assault that, very quickly, will draw them in much, much deeper."

I sit there stunned, shuffling through presentation charts on the screen.

"Don, on the last employee conference call, you said our purpose was social engagement, ultimately. Educating young people about climate change. Like, the idea that games deepen our connections to one another, where we learn about others and ourselves, where artificial conflict itself can shape moral outlook."

"The world is a little more complex than a corporate purpose statement. There are realities out there we need to be mindful of."

"Like what?"

He smirks, then. "You're being willfully naive." He pauses to give me a once-over, then: "Joanna, there's a great future for you in this company if you open your eyes and your heart to what we're really doing. We can discuss this over dinner when we land."

A colleague back at the lab warned me to expect the dinner invitation at which he'll inevitably suggest — or so I'm told — that we'll need to go up to his suite to work on the presentation. I've heard he's got booty-call girls all over the company.

After I step off the plane onto the runway, I lug my garment bag through the jet engine hum, followed by the customs guy, who only glances at my passport. The air is humid with rain and fog, metallic with exhaust.

I keep walking.

In the taxi, alone, I email my resignation to HR.

Second memory, a year later:

As I approach the door of my condo, I'm rooting around for my keys while continuing to scroll my phone, which surfaces a new text from Rajiv, a trusted colleague at the start-up I joined after leaving Greenhouse.

> Hey do you know about the partner discussions with the pharma guys. Our Dear Leader has been in meetings with them on the sly. Are you in on this? If you are, I have a real problem. Talk tomorrow!

I'm too exhausted to reply other than with a stunned-face emoji.

Inside, I kick off my heels before lighting incense sticks in each corner of the living room. Arriving home after a long day at work requires activity to tame anxieties inflamed by the daily psychological consequences of entrepreneurial chaos in a start-up. In the kitchen, I grab a veggie juice from the rack and put it to chill. I then lazily take a Peloton class, during which I climb into the Swiss Alps, helped along by a Lady Gaga playlist. Dinner is Uber Eats — vegan steak, washed down with a homeopathic remedy I'm hopeful will reduce my stress levels without leading me back into drugs.

Before bed, I have inconclusive phone sex with an online friend I've never met in person who, tonight, identifies as a Black woman, although I preferred our last encounter, when my friend identified as a white corporate male who likes to be spanked.

The next morning, at a diner around the corner from the office, I meet Rajiv alone for breakfast, a habit we've gotten into for trading gossip.

"I'm not sure what to say," I say as the waitress refills our coffees. "All along, we said this was a natural health–based educational app, holistic, no meds."

"Yeah, well, he's talking to the pharma guys. Alone. We gotta stop this."

I admire Rajiv's fearlessness, especially given that he's a skinny little guy, maybe five six, a bucktooth smile dominating a brown face. Twice a week he brings his mother into the office and, in a sari, speaking Hindi and little else, she whips up curry meals for the software developers working through the night.

"Rajiv, let's not jump off a bridge here. We're doing God's work."

"God has nothing to do with this."

"It will all work out. I'm pretty confident."

"Then why do you spend hours in the bathroom, in tears, scrolling Instagram for cat videos, for all I know."

"How do you know what I'm doing in the bathroom?"

"Well, I'm a surveillance networking expert."

"Rajiv!"

"Relax. I'd never track you. But I've seen you come back to your office with your mascara smeared like some blind person tried to paint a clown face on you."

"Some days are better than others."

In theory we work in an egalitarian, progressive workplace. But I'm on edge more than usual these days because, as the Finance VP managing our upcoming IPO process, I'm a frequent target for the unhinged rages of the Founder.

"Anyway, it wouldn't be cat videos," I say. "That's your thing."

"Actually, it's not cat videos that break my heart. It's *inter-species* love that gets me. Cats and humans. A raccoon cuddling with a dog. A dove sitting on a horse."

"And, of course, there's you and me."

I've speculated on what a platonic marriage would be like to Rajiv, who has only recently come out. Would we each take lovers? Share one? If there's been one saving grace to the nightmare of start-up life, it's been his unflappability, his skillful use of humour to deflect any verbal assault from company bullies when delays happen in getting the new app ready. He'll make a wonderful father one day.

"So back to the pharma question," he says, slicing into his omelette. "Are you on board against the meds thing? Nowhere do you exclude the medical angle, in the latest version of our story and in the investor documents."

"You're catastrophizing."

"There's a gap a mile wide in the story where meds can come into play. This is clearly fucked up. It's sort of dog-whistling to those pharma assholes."

"The prospectus mentions nothing directly."

"Directly? Joanna, the app is for *children*."

Later that day:

"Run that by me again," the Founder says, after his attention-deficit moment at his workstation, where he has completed six trades on three different exchanges.

I've trained myself not to react emotionally or angrily to the Founder's inability to stay in the moment with me or anyone except an investor. Still, it's hard to sit here with him and not want to slap this black-turtleneck-wearing, barefoot-in-loafers techno-nerd, this Steve Jobs wannabe.

I say, "We've told the schools and clinicians that the app would feature natural health solutions to go with the learning modules. But not prescribed meds."

"Well, our valuation will triple if we get meds into the solution. We need to keep all possibilities open to generate value out of the gate."

I lean back in my chair and, briefly, wish I had the audacity to cross and uncross my legs, allowing my skirt to ride up my thighs to give my tantrum-prone CEO a brief, unrequited look at what he wants but I won't give, no matter how much he corners and harasses me. Instead, I lean forward, drain my face of everything except the earnestness that arises out of my well-tuned *pleaser* persona, a character trait that my current therapist says prevents me from developing healthy relationships.

"You know I came here to change the world," I say, convincingly.

"That's my girl."

"I'm not your fucking girl."

He smiles at the profanity that he believes, rightly, is an act to show that I'm one of the guys, hey, just a bro with great tits, yeah, with a mouth on her that can suck the chrome right off a trailer hitch.

Mostly I treat Dear Leader as if he were an annoying kid brother who insists on being pacified with an endless stream of gifts that, daily, I deliver by reporting on the progress toward each milestone involved in taking the company public. Not yet forty and already worth half a billion, the Founder has, for this start-up, his third, leaned into presenting a neurodivergent persona to investors, claiming in his presentations that he's not only ADHD but dyslexic and OCD, unable to read, exclusively an oral learner, and therefore uniquely qualified to help millions of children globally learn better and faster with the new app, NxtScool. I know better, having watched him spend hours closely editing the dense documents in the due diligence binders while we flew on his jet to meet the sovereign fund managers in Riyadh. On that flight, when I wondered aloud whether investors might prefer a more businesslike CEO rather than the classic techno-nerd, he told me that all tech billionaires need to come off like sociopathic weirdos.

As I stand to leave, he says, "Tonight I want a look at the revised prospectus."

"I'll bring it over to your place."

"You bet."

After work, I find myself in the crowded streets of Kensington Market, relishing the aromas of a dozen food cultures mingling with weed vapour and loudspeaker reggae. A classic midsummer night in the city where it seems every second person is half-naked, stripped down to sports bras and singlets. I feel older than I want to be. I wonder where my twenties went, the years after MBA school before the career took off, doing things I guess I'll never, ever do again: a line of coke snorted off my boyfriend's penis during a relapse, trading stocks with insider info, acting on a girlfriend's dare and actually dancing for an entire night in a cage in a strip club. The shit I got up to.

Lost in thought, I walk past the taco joint until Rajiv, on the patio, calls out.

"That pitcher of margarita looks inviting," I say. "But, you know, recovery."

"Why are you dressed like Cinderella going to the ball?"

"I'm meeting with Dear Leader to go over the prospectus. His place."

"Wow, you're taking ass-kissing to a literal level."

"I need a favour from you."

"If you're going to fuck him, you don't need my help."

"Rajiv," I say, softly. "Do you trust me?"

An hour later, I'm going up the elevator to the penthouse, a soundless adventure that showcases the amazing city views. The elevator opens directly into his unit, decorated as a Turkish spa, the walls and floors covered in shimmering carpets with abstracted floral designs, the living room empty of furniture except silk cushions on the floor, the air alive with melancholic Middle Eastern music. He's alone, as I expected, sitting in a corner, cross-legged, vaping while scrolling his phone.

"Joanna," he says, not looking up. "We have things to discuss, together."

I allow nature to take its course. Mostly. With props.

A week later, I eavesdrop on two of our senior app developers who huddle over a screen in the lounge area, watching the video clip making the global rounds.

"Do we even have a clue who made this video?"

"Look at that motherfucker. Our CEO — well, former CEO."

"What's she doing to him?"

"That's gotta hurt. Is he even awake? Looks out of it."

"I get it. Some dudes, not just women, you know, like to be spanked."

"Shut the fuck up."

"Live and let live, fine. But tell me something. Would you want your mother to know you're going around with some kind of furry tail sticking out of your butt?"

"I mean fun is fun. But this shit — wow, like, you can't unsee it after seeing it."

"Think they knew there was a video drone outside the window?"

"Who the fuck knows?"

"Well, it looks like a set-up to me. Someone wanted that guy fired. It's all over the fucking internet right now. Isn't it? Try taking a company public with this out there."

"Look at that shit she's doing to him. They're breaking the laws of physics or something. Seriously, is the dude out cold?"

"The girl. Serious tits."

"Wonder what the face looks like."

"Digital blurring. We'll never know."

A month later:

My phone goes off.

"Rajiv. What's up?"

"Where are you?"

I'm staring out at distant, snow-topped mountains striving against the Nepalese sky. I feel Rajiv in my energy bubble as a gentle swirl of warm colours.

Closing my eyes, I'm sure I can see him as he can't see himself.

He says, "Can we, like, meet? I mean, really clear this up. I need you back here."

"You're the new CEO, Rajiv. Your video drones did it! We got our Dear Leader fired. And without his compensation package, either. Now you're the boss."

"I didn't think you'd bail, though. I also didn't think you'd fuck him. And, by the looks of it, you slipped something into his drink."

"He was committed to the pharma story. Technically, there was no fucking. It was simulated, the humping. Undignified, but what's done is done."

"We could both go to prison for this."

"Now you can do things your way. So do it. Save the children, as you say."

There's a long pause.

"I need you back here," he says. "We have a business to build."

"I'm where I should be, Rajiv. At some point, my options will vest. That's good enough for me. So, help the children. Do it right."

"Joanna, I can't do this without you."

"Rajiv, I'm on a different journey."

Third memory:

They threaten to slice my perineum to make room for the baby's head. I tell them no fucking way — that's barbaric. So, the midwife says, Push harder, now.

It's pain beyond what I imagined it would ever be.

At first, both Clare and Ray are in the room with me, going through the verbal coaching motions in a spirited way they learned from our prenatal consultant.

I send them away in a rage.

I've also had enough of doing the birthing in a wading pool. They take me to a bed surrounded by technology to monitor whatever's happening to me and the baby.

God, how I suck down the nitrous oxide. Originally I said, *No drugs*, the risk too high for falling off the wagon. But I'm sucking away every chance I get.

Eventually, there's progress. Pain with purpose.

And everybody's in the room now for the final push —

Then Rosa in my arms.

Oh, the screams. What a cranky little beast!

Clare and Ray, hands joined, cut the cord. They remind me of politicians at a ribbon-cutting ceremony, doing what's necessary but not much more.

The doctors want to take the baby away to do some testing. I say no fucking way. These are important moments, when a mother needs to be connected to her child.

Clare and Ray take baby selfies while I'm being cleaned up.

Later, in the recovery suite we built into the family villa, I'm finally alone with Rosa, who is snoring on my naked chest after gurgling down a hefty amount of breast milk.

Her little heart beating.

I hear Clare in the garden, giving a seminar to her group of acolytes, which seems to double in size every month. She's in charge, or needs to be, always. She has the controlling instincts of a cult leader and the charm, too. She wants a bigger community for taking her spiritual practice to the next level.

Ray is off somewhere, doing his nightly micro-dosing which, I have come to believe, is macro-dosing and troublingly habitual, although he denies it.

I hear the sea outside.

After a few days of mother-daughter recovery time, it's clear I'm depressed and volatile or, classically, I guess, I'm in the postpartum depression zone.

I understand what's happening to me. I will recover. And do, soon, with the help of our homeopath, herbalist, and acupuncturist. The blackness recedes while emotional balance arrives. There's just one problem, which a hormonal tweaking and more sleep can't solve. I know I don't belong here in this utopian island enclave, no matter how sovereign we are, no matter how coddled I am in our polyamorous remove.

Old anger has surfaced in me, which cancels out the new love I feel for Rosa.

Anger at everything that made me.

All the biases inflicted on me from the moment I was Rosa's age.

Anger that needs a stage.

Stop this, Joanna! Stop with the memories. Come back to the present!

And so I do.

More often than not, I do everything I can to stay in the present. Otherwise, the allure of a self-inflicted death surges within me.

So, I must leave these memories behind right now.

Here on this plane, as I slouch the hours away after my short and probably last visit with Rosa and her guardians, I tell myself I don't want to die. That I have something to live for. A child. Then why have I left? Perhaps I do want to die.

What I say or believe is not the same as what I do.

My purpose isn't a fire burnt down to embers. It's barely been lit.

So many know there's a lot systemically wrong in society but feel helpless to do anything but grumble or lash out at scapegoats, often those the most vulnerable. It's far easier to moan into our media feeds, where so many of us are plainly lost in conspiracy theory and corporate misinformation, or simplistic arguments about what's wrong and who's responsible. Our society is sick and getting sicker, epidemically so. And angrier.

Still, for most people, the incendiary conclusion that everything in our society should be burned down is not a welcome or legitimate choice.

Am I insane?

Or is my burden an excess of sanity?

It is so easy to go over the edge.

I've marched around with militias in fatigues and night-vision headsets. I've withheld taxes on anarchist principles. I exist on the sharpest edge of the rebellion spectrum, not just the theatre of it, not just virtue-signalling or cancelling others. I've taken to the streets and fought through pepper spray, rubber bullets, truncheons.

I'm a warrior for change who will inevitably underestimate the costs of tearing down one world to rebuild it to my utopian specifications.

I have had people killed: corporatized victimizers, especially, and their enablers.

I've abandoned my daughter, in the here and now.

May this be love, even if conceived in hate.

Don

For hours we sit there, risking our sanity by calling up memories of the early years with Tony, all the stress and wonder of that time, the panic every new parent endures. We dredge up the smallest episodes in our dead family romance that only Lily and I know about, the in-between moments, when Tony uttered his first word, took his first step, got stitches, fell asleep in my arms while I droned through *Goodnight Moon*.

If this is torture, it's the torture we both need right now.

Then the notification hits my phone, taking nearly two minutes to decrypt.

I feel like I'm dying while a chessboard forms on my console screen, requiring me to start a game with whoever's on the other end.

"I have no fucking idea what's going on here," I say. "I'm a decent chess player. The other side, black, is playing to lose. It's a verification riff, I guess."

After I lock in the easy checkmate move, another box opens on my screen with instructions to click. And another notification comes into my headset.

Eris: One more test and we'll take you to your son.

GM001: What more do you want?

Eris: We need a safe place here to satisfy my request.

GM001: Well, you're gonna have to evade game Security.

Eris: Why can't you call them off?

GM001: The board has given you money. That's their limit.

Eris: Then we'll have to hide where they can't find us.

GM001: Good luck doing that.

Eris: We know this game as well as you do, if not better.

GM001: Let's see, then.

I turn to Lily, who is hovering behind me.

"Okay," I say, too calmly. "We're going on a little trip together."

"What?"

"You need to come with me."

I motion for her to plug into my grandmaster console.

"You're kidding," she says.

"Put this on," I say, handing her an experimental, next-gen headset.

Tony

I awaken and know instantly I'm on a plane, in flight.

Where the fuck am I? With whom? Where am I going?

Lily

Once he lowers the headset onto me, everything is spectacularly different. I'm presented with an intensely deep field of vision in the compressed interior space of a bright, windowed room, a simulation of an air traffic control tower. Beyond the windows there are runways in all directions across an empty vista.

Eris: Look ahead.

A huge dot, a black ball of a thing, materializes over a runway that vanishes into a horizon. This is what's speaking to me and Don.

Eris: Come now, we need privacy, then all will end well.

And through the windows we proceed, no broken glass, just us in the air, floating above the landscape. As we approach, the black ball recedes while rising higher in the sky. We follow at some distance as the runways below fall away from us both.

LB001: Where to?
GM001: Just follow.

Eris is moving faster now, the view impressively realistic, as are the sound and console effects. I feel like I'm piloting a plane and it's exciting and frightening at once.

Suddenly, there's a savage flash near the horizon, a vertical line of orange from the ground to the top of the visible atmosphere. And then everything goes dark, except for this vertical stripe of orange that we're racing toward. Seconds later, we enter something apocalyptic, because there's no other word for it: a tunnel of fire. And this, too, feels glorious, a bath in the vibrant and the subtle, the solar field visuals so varied, streaky, a burning orange in so many colours doing so many things.

Whatever I am — and I'm not sure what I am here — is tethered to the black ball moving through the heatless flame. My stomach flip-flops as we go into a hard descent. And fall we do, so fast I'm going to pass out, and then I think I have passed out, because it's all faded to black. But it's not me. We're diving into actual black.

LB001: Where are we?
GM001: Inside an oil spill.

We surface onto an oil-rig platform on an oily blue-black sea. The scene landward is coastal. A beach, palm trees, dunes. Around the platform in the water are sea animals, turtles, dolphins, brown pelicans. All oil-slicked, all floating, dead.

For a few minutes, nothing happens, other than the rocking sensation of being at sea, the memory of incipient seasickness. I close my eyes and the sensation deepens.

I half expect to hear my mother whispering, *Here, dear, some flat ginger ale, it'll settle your tummy.* The dead sea creatures are beautifully rendered.

Eris: Some members love playing dead, out of respect.

LB001: If this is fun for them, I can't say I'd understand.

GM001: My data vitals say Security is not far behind.

Eris: Then we need to keep moving.

Clouds blossom overhead, squirting instantly into view by some hidden force, taking shape as if an invisible pastry chef were frosting blobs on a giant blue cake. As upset as I am, as confused and disoriented as I am, what Don and his designers have created here is wonderfully psychedelic, to use an old-fashioned word. Just enough is real here that the surreal doesn't seem fake. I can see why some people never want to leave, and become addicted to living in unreal places like this.

Eris: Don, are the clouds a Security unit?

GM001: I'm afraid so.

LB001: I want my boy. I will do anything.

Eris: We need to move.

The platform dissolves into a depthless black chasm into which we soon start to sink. Seconds later, we emerge into a pink-ribbed cavern or tunnel system. It's as if we've been swallowed by a whale. We come to a complete stop above a conveyor of sorts, which turns out to be a line of barrels — or industrial drums, also in pink — all jammed together, extending in both directions as far as my eyes can see.

LB001: What is this place?

Eris: It is an unexplored secret in the game.

GM001: It presents as toxic waste that poisons the surface.

LB001: Excuse me?

GM001: Members who come here or live above it — they get sick, die.

LB001: For God's sake.

Eris: The truth of who we are is not always pleasant.

LB001: What do you want from me, from us?

A drilling noise over us.

Eris: Security is nearly here — time to move again.

We're spinning now, drilling down, corkscrewing through whatever's here. It's very strange. Like a flight simulator, I would imagine, Don's gamemaster console pitches and yaws and vibrates and moves in ways that make you feel that your actions — or the weather, or the machine you control — have consequences. It's designed to make you feel superhero-powerful, capable of controlling forces that you can't logically control.

The next leg of the journey is chaotic, involving a lot of stopping and starting, as if we're exploring options, making decisions on the fly. For about an hour, we rampage through one game landscape after another. At times we burst into crowds of activity, into fighting and killing against backdrops of explosions and destructive mayhem. Just when I think we're about to settle into an area, we veer off and charge into new visuals. Eris is having trouble keeping distance from whatever is chasing us.

At last, we stop. It's an open-pit mine. A giant, terraced hole of ugliness, raging in dust storms and patrolled by massive dump trucks.

Eris: Asbestos.

LB001: The game knows history.

Eris: We're in Canada.

LB001: My home and native land.

Eris: Where they ship asbestos to the developing world.

LB001: Why are we here?

Eris: It is a safe place to end our discussion.

GM001: We have a few minutes at most — so what's the deal?

Eris: I'll show you him, alive. To prove this is in good faith.

My voice doesn't feel like it's my own, but I'm screaming now. The black ball turns to white, exploding white from within.

And there he is, it's him, within the white circle, our boy, lying on a bunk bed in a small room. The video is grainy, but I'm sure it's him.

LB001: Don, is this live? Or a recording?

GM001: The data vitals say it's a live feed. But he's not on the ground.

Eris: He's on a plane, flying to you. We are, together.

GM001: Sorry.

Eris: We moved him to another jurisdiction to avoid tracking.

GM001: How do we close this deal?

Eris: There's a van arriving outside your building. Tell your security detail not to track you. Or else, understand? With our faraday zone patterns, you will be brought to a meeting point where your son will be released. If you are tracked, and we'll know if you are, your son's life ... need I say more.

Jun

I've lost control —

Will the game, our business, be destroyed?

Who is going to die?

Eris

They're in the van, where I'll leave them alone — for now.

I take no pleasure in tormenting the parents. But I'm well defended against the impulse to let pity rule. So many millions of members out there need me. How many wasting their lives, unable to stop living in the game and paying rent to these parasites? But what are the odds of the plane going undetected for much longer?

Will this be the end for me?

Regardless, our team in Nigeria tells me we have enough time to deploy our malware in the game. It all depends on Don Barton giving us entry to the member module engine, which is the most protected of everything his teams have built.

And once our malware is in the game, in tens of millions of computers ...

It will spread across the world.

There's nothing to say until they clear any localized tracking risks so that we can be certain, or reasonably certain, that we can land and depart again uncontested.

We're in the air, circling and circling.

Nothing to indicate our plane or their van is being tracked. Yet.

Inside the game:

Eris: Take me into the game's crown jewels.

GM001: Sorry?

Eris: Please.

GM001: Please what?

Eris: You're being tedious. We need to do a global update to the global member engine. Change all their profiles.

GM001: Security won't let that happen.

Eris: You can override Security. You're a gamemaster.

GM001: Why not just destroy the game itself?

Eris: Because you can rebuild it. Please, stop being stupid.

GM001: You want to infect each user, their avatars? Do you understand what that could cause?

Eris: It is ransomware of a kind. You've paid it before.

GM001: We've given you a hundred million. You want to fleece our customers personally, the kids? Haven't you taken enough?

Eris: Oh, this has nothing to do with more money. We want — how shall I put it — the members to do our bidding in the world.

GM001: Whatever you have in mind, I can't let you do that.

Eris: Lily, talk to your husband. Save your son's life.

GM001: You'd kill him?

In the cabin behind me, the boy is pounding on the locked door.

He's recovering fast from the drugging.

I check in with the radar guys. All good. The plane may not have the latest surveillance tech, but it's good enough to assess who's coming after us.

So far, so good.

Eris: I need an entry link.

My console pings with an entry link to the Greenhouse global update module, which I forward to the malware guys, who may or may not be in Syria or Laos.

GM001: Satisfied?

That's when, out of the porthole, I see the escorts. Fighter jets. No identifying symbols. Not much to do other than continue on.

Eris: You're putting everyone in danger, you realize.
GM001: What are you talking about?
Eris: You know exactly what.
GM001: No, I don't.
Eris: We have a tail up here. They could blow us out of the sky.
GM001: We had nothing to do with that.

The malware guys say that there are precisely 46,375,401 players in the game currently. All infection targets. The world won't be the same tomorrow. Forty-six-plus million people whose digital lives and assets ... infected. Perhaps we'll throw in a video meme, featuring Don confessing, admitting that his goal was ultimately youth addiction. Even if the clip isn't fully authentic. Just a little bit of deep-fake news, a collage. Which doesn't matter. The point is, we will have destroyed his life's work.

And forty-six million infections will become two billion soon enough.

Patience.

Don

I'm not sure how he's done it, but Bai Jun has come into the game undetected by Eris, wherever she is. On the van console I see his face, under which his executive icon glows. There's a chat box open and whoever's typing for him makes it clear that I'm to say nothing, that a special operation is in progress that will resolve the situation.

Lily nearly gives Bai Jun away with a shout but catches herself, and turns the shout into a wail, a crying jag. It's an act. She appears to pull it off.

Eris has just disabled all my outgoing comm systems, including my watch. She must know now that Bai Jun has entered the scene. But the compass app on my phone is still working. We've been heading north for a few hours now. No longer on the main highway. It's a bumpy rural road. Then we come to a halt.

GM001: Where are you? Where are we?

The doors open.

We're in the middle of nowhere, on a highway with only trees on all sides. The van headlights don't go very far before darkness kills them off. It's cold. Neither of us is properly dressed for this. To our left, through the trees, I glimpse a long line of white lights at ground level, which immediately gets me thinking — given all the corporate-jet travel I've done — that there's a runway over there. I grab Lily's hand and we pick our way, stumbling, through the trees. Turns out I'm right. It's some kind of makeshift airport with only a Quonset hut for a terminal, unlit, no one there, and two fuel trucks. The runway itself is in perfect condition, just long enough for a mid-sized private jet, in my estimation, and lit with enough wattage to settle any pilot's nerves.

In the distance, perhaps a kilometre away, a plane descends toward us, and lands seconds later. It's a sonic nightmare until the plane stops a stone's throw from us, although its engines keep whining. It's a small but advanced Cessna Citation. I know because it's on the short list of planes I'm thinking of buying for myself.

"My God," Lily yells behind me, before running toward the plane.

"Lily, hold on — we don't know who's on that plane."

She comes to a stop in front of the cockpit, hands on her hips.

That's when I notice the armed men in paramilitary gear emerging from the trees. Must be ten of them or more. Are these Bai Jun's guys? Who the fuck are they?

The interior lights of the plane go dark. The cockpit door opens and lets down a step. Then a woman appears at the open door. It's hard to tell but she looks to be in her thirties, slim, dressed in athletic gear, blond, hair braided down her back. There's a sleek red harness of some type — maybe a bulletproof vest — on her chest.

"You're Eris," I say.

"You've come with some friends, I see."

"I don't know who these guys are."

"Where's our son?" Lily says, starting to climb the stairs.

But the women motions for her to stop, saying, "Your son will come out alive, but don't come any farther until I explain something. Or we'll all die."

"All die?"

"This vest is a bomb. I can detonate it with a voice command."

"We just want our son," Lily says. "Alive."

"I want to get out of here alive," Eris says. "But your friends with the big guns here may not agree to anything."

None of the armed men gives any indication of anything. They just surround the plane.

"So here's what I propose," Eris says. "Don and Lily, you will join me on the plane for a minute or two. And if your friends want to attack, we'll all die. But hopefully sanity will prevail and, safely, we can bring this to an end."

Tony

I hear voices — some screaming. It's my mom, shouting my name. And now she's pounding on the door. I hear electronic beeps — must be the lock code to my cabin. And then the door opens. Mum basically tackles me backward into the bunk, where we flop down together, her yelling my name and squeezing the air out of me.

My dad's in the main cabin, peering at us, and behind him there's a woman. Must be Eris. And whatever the fuck she's wearing over her workout gear I don't want to know. So as my dad comes forward to join us, I ask Eris what's up.

"It's an explosive device."

"You gonna blow us the fuck up?"

Eris motions for me and Mum to come toward her. As we do, she pushes us toward the open door and we tumble down the retractable steps, down onto the road, surrounded by these heavy dudes with guns.

"Don, where are you?" Mum yells.

But my father doesn't appear. Instead the steps rise again into the belly of the plane and the door locks shut. While we're standing there, the plane revs up, executes a sharp turn, and rockets down the runway and up into the sky, banking out of sight.

Lily

We're ushered into the van by the armed men, all face-masked. I presume they're men. But I'm soon corrected. There's a woman's voice that I recognize, or think I do. There's just enough of her wavy black hair escaping her helmet that I can confirm my suspicions. It's the corporate psychologist who accused Don of kidnapping Tony.

In the van, she joins us, sitting in the front.

"It's you again, isn't it?" I say. "Who are you, anyway?"

The mask stares back at me.

So I continue, "Are you here with permission from any government? Anyone?"

Nothing.

"Mum, what's up?" Tony blinks in a wide-eyed stutter, as if he were just waking up, or about to collapse.

"Tony, you played a terrible game with us."

"Can we go home now?"

The three-hour ride downtown is uneventful, providing plenty of time for me to issue predictable banalities to my son. I mention something about a holiday. I cheerily go on and on about how Tina, his dog, misses him so much, sleeping on his bed at night. I sense Tony is caught between his need to shelter himself in my relief that he's returned alive and another force equal to it, his fear that once we get home, in the privacy of the condo, I'll hand down punishment — no gaming, no friends, curfew, no nothing, forever; tutors hired overnight in math, science, every subject. For all I know, he may be charged criminally, although I'm hoping his father and Bai Jun won't let that happen.

"You're fidgeting, Tony."

He glares at me. "Could I borrow your phone, Mum? Just check in with my friends."

Unbelievable.

Already he's seeing the possibility — the hope — of normality orchestrating again.

I haven't given Don a second thought since we got in the van. He might be dead now, for all I know.

Jun

I wait, alone, behind a desk that many have walked toward nervously or, often enough, visibly fearful. Once a favour-seeker broke wind on approach and fainted away. The tears of middle-aged executives have spattered my black marble floor, tarnishing its polished mirror sheen. I've stopped distraught women from disrobing, as if somehow a decision of mine would change after an exposed breast or a sloppily painted mouth gaped toward me while trembling hands moved to unbuckle me.

I've had the most difficult cases restrained by Security and taken away to the helicopter on the roof and then to a fate I'd rather not think about right now.

I've lived and worked in the sky for years, in this suite high above West Kowloon, where on some days I look down at clouds. Below me, most of the buildings look like toys that can be moved by executive whim. Same with the views of the ships in the water.

Years have also been spent working day and night on my plane, shuttling between continents and business operations. Time zones mattered little. I recognize the dangers of the sky perspective and the presumption of godlike reach.

The American finally appears, a white cable flowing from his head to the phone in hand, his gaze looking past me while he conducts a conversation in Spanish with heated diversions in Cantonese. All I can make out is that Don and the terrorists are being tracked in the plane and there is no consensus, yet, on how to bring the situation to an end, safely or otherwise.

I begged him to protect Don and his family. But the matter is out of my hands.

So I wait. Clearly, he intends for me to wait.

He wanders the room with unkempt élan, his blue tie askew, loose at the neck, a white shirttail about to emerge at a hip, his suit off the rack, the shoes thick-soled and scuffed at the heels. He might be in his late thirties.

For a good ten minutes, he stands close to the windows, his back turned to me. My time has evidently come. I'm a god no more.

Others appear, a tense group of my retainers alongside his.

After his phone conversation ends, he saunters over to sit on the edge of my desk. Without a glance at me, he says, "We wish you well in all your future endeavours."

When he finally looks at me, the eyes have nothing to say.

"Don Barton. What's being done to protect him?"

"You have other things to worry about."

I knew this moment would come one day. It always comes.

My preparations involved nothing more than a reminder to myself to not reach for files or computers or personal mementoes to take with me.

I come around to shake his hand. His grip is firm but the palm's moist — too moist.

"Don't be nervous," I whisper in Chinese.

This angers him but he swallows the comment. The handshake goes on too long, but neither of us want to retreat first. Such bullshit. I'm too old for this.

He says, "I understand your daughter has been accepted into graduate school."

This angers me but I restrain myself. "As part of my separation agreement, you are to terminate all collateral surveillance of my family and closest associates."

"A deal is a deal."

I'm not sure he knows, or would even care, that whoever takes over this office is inheriting a desk that once belonged to Mao himself. At least that's the claim from the auction house. Will they even look at the Yuan ink drawings along the back wall?

A Chinese national has been tapped to lead the Greenhouse business in Asia. I've known him for years as the lapdog to the senior leaders at State Security. As for the rest of our world markets, it's an American who will guide the Greenhouse business, a person who is also well known in the intelligence community.

The American pulls the shoulder-caress trick, leading me over to the window.

"Bai Jun, you've been a corporate warrior of a kind for a long time. I know this isn't the way you would have preferred to leave."

"It is better than being buried with my possessions prematurely."

He gives me a strange look. "That could be arranged, if you prefer."

He means this as a joke. I accept it as such.

"Bai Jun, you have created enormous value and now you are being repaid, or you will be once the transaction to take Greenhouse private closes. As it shortly will."

"I see no reason for shareholders to turn their backs on the offer."

"In this situation, it is far better for Greenhouse to be run as a private company, beholden only to its owners, not the public markets."

My eyes, I hope, betray nothing. My sources inform me that the money involved in taking Greenhouse private comes from off-the-books resources held by Chinese and American security operatives. They also tell me that, contrary to early reports, there *was* a global malware attack executed against the game and its nearly fifty million users. Except it wasn't done by the hackers but by our new Security team as a government-sanctioned infection, initiated by the Chinese and Americans acting together.

If I say this aloud, though, I will end up in a grave without my possessions.

That Greenhouse becomes a laboratory for global surveillance, that it will track users unaware, that infected users will eventually spread the malware infection to billions: All this I cannot stop, as much as it disgusts me.

It's time to make an exit and open my golden parachute.

"I know you don't think very highly of us, Bai Jun. Or of me."

"It isn't personal. It is a larger ethical question."

"Yet you tried very hard to get me and this deal undone, going so far as to speak to your Politburo friend. About me, especially. For what, interrogating and slapping you around for a few hours? Seems childish, given the money you're making here."

"It turns out your friends have more influence."

He pulls out an envelope from his suit and dangles it. "If you want it."

"To what do I owe this last gesture of hospitality?"

"For years you've told anyone who would listen that your parents were executed for crimes against the Party they did not commit."

"It is what I was told as a boy, by my aunt."

"You should have been more vigilant in your investigations. Your parents were agitators by the day's standards. Anti-government, anti-Communist."

"You speak with such confidence."

"It doesn't matter to me what they did or didn't do, Bai Jun," he says, baring his perfect American teeth, whitened beyond white. "What matters is who turned them in."

It's all I can do not to reach for his throat.

"It's all in the envelope. Verifiable information."

"Why are you doing this? It can't be to benefit me in any way."

"We have an expression about people who think they're superior to you ... *your shit doesn't stink.*"

He gestures as if ready to put the envelope away again, then says, "I can take this away with me, if you like. But I know you want it. Let's see how committed you are to larger ethical questions, as you so eloquently put it."

Eris

In flight, Don and I sit directly across from one another. But he's not paying the slightest attention to me while scrolling his phone. It's amazing, this act, pretending to be calm. I want to see how long he can keep up this old-school corporate bullshit.

He gives me a sarcastic glare, then. "Let me tell you where I am. I've just been removed from the board of directors of the company I founded. Our stock has dropped almost fifty percent, because of rumours of the malware attack you're unleashing."

"I find it disturbing that business is what's on your mind right now."

He laughs. "My legal team has also advised me that the American security authorities have opened a cyberterrorism investigation. And I'm a suspect."

"Well, you are cybercriminal, in a different sense."

"The anti-media, anti-capitalist fanatic. Your generation's Ulrike Meinhof."

"There are similarities."

"What she wanted for West Germany, you want for the entire world. The question is, will you commit suicide when your revolution doesn't come to pass?"

"Death comes to us all. Picking a time of one's choosing isn't the worst option."

"Bullshit," he says. No anger in his voice, just an eerie calmness.

"Well. It's going to be a long flight before we set you free."

"I suspect you'll keep me in suspense about our destination."

"A security protocol, yes."

With that, he goes back to his phone.

There's a decommissioned military base up north where we'll refuel before the long, circuitous trip to Myanmar. The country — or failing state, actually — is the current base for one of the hacker teams that does contract work for us: mostly Russian and Serbian expats. They've cut a deal on our behalf with the generals in power to give our group safe haven. It's exorbitantly expensive, requiring more than half our crypto reserves. And it's definitely not a permanent situation. But it's all we have. Pretty much every other failed or failing state we investigated couldn't guarantee our safety, or we couldn't trust them not to turn us over to the Americans or Chinese.

"Don, one more thing: Who were these armed mercenaries who approached our plane on our arrival? They're likely not your people. Which government?"

He thinks about that but says, wearily, "It's hard to know where our company ends and the government begins. Or where one government ends and another begins."

"Sounds like a conspiracy theory to me."

"You're a real piece of work," he says, suddenly hostile. "You manipulated my son. Threatened his life — a threat to be taken seriously, as you've taken the lives of others in the name of whatever insane vision you're chasing. You want to take us back to the Stone Age. To grass huts. How deluded you people are. How evil."

"I think you're more worried about the game than your son."

"Fuck you."

"Your son, I think, may have a new perspective on his father."

"And what's next? Throw me out of the plane? Kill us both with your bomb?"

"You're the hostage, and the only reason we haven't been blown out of the air. Be assured, we will release you at our final destination."

He looks at me differently, evidently shocked. "Are you who I think you might be?"

"Who might that be?"

"You've had surgery, but it's you. Joanna something or other."

"Not bad."

"So is this revenge? For what?"

"Let's not make a tiny corporate melodrama the story here," I say. "I'm not going to say that knowing you wasn't added motivation. You helped me get on this path, but I wouldn't make too much of that. That's your ego speaking."

"You're insane."

"Don, your technologies and your games have stolen our energy, everything that connects us to each other, to the planet. And for me the question is Why?"

"You're fucking nuts."

When he finally notices the jets, he asks who's tracking us.

"I don't know, not for sure."

Other than it has to be an intelligence agency. Borders no longer dictate who's involved here. What is clear is that we've been compromised by informants or moles.

How much Don knows about this, who knows? But then the alert comes in. Oh my: Our malware guys are all dead or in custody, the malware attack prevented.

No time to think as bullets shatter porthole glass and rip into the cabin.

Don

I wake up in the smouldering wreckage. The plane is more or less intact, the engines still whirring. There's a fire somewhere. Smell of burning plastics.

I look out the broken window. It's a snowy, flat landscape. Bitterly cold now.

I look down to my chest, covered in blood. I've been shot somewhere but I don't feel anything except the warmth of the blood.

Where did she go?

Sirens.

I see the snowdrifts off the runway turning red — not with blood but the reflection of lights from emergency vehicles surrounding the plane.

Tony

At the condo for only an hour, and I'm sick. I feel sick.

There's a part of me that wants to jump out of the window, or scream or do something, or fly like I normally do in the game, kicking ass, racing around alien worlds, destroying shit, crashing through buildings, and leaping over oceans and deserts — all that and more.

I want to live in the game. And yet. I feel the ache trembling through my fingers, behind my eyes, in my restless legs. I'm talking to myself, repeating to myself what the therapist in the van said: *Just do the next right thing; don't think of tomorrow or next week.* But this minute, I need to find my way into the game. I need to stay outside the game. I so want to run free and wild and be someone else, lost in adventures so much more engaging than anything and anyone in the here and now.

I can't do this on my own.

What is the next best thing?

Lily

From a hospital bed, a week after the operation, Don says, weakly, "My lawyers — well, one group of them — now tell me the Americans may back off, if and only if we play this right, but we still have to prove the game is not hiding any cyberterrorists."

"Will the game be taken down?"

"No, but someone is forcing a sale of the company, taking it private at twice the current stock price. Who knows why this is happening. Bai Jun has gone silent."

"Financially, isn't it true we're making a killing on the sale?"

"That is true. Tell me something, where is the boy right now?"

"In his room most of the day. Says he's reading. Not playing the game."

"Not that he can get in, not after what I've done."

"How can you be so certain?"

"I can't."

Jun

I'm basking in glorious sunshine on the private patio of my meditation shack in the tea-growing hills behind Longjing. This will be my residential base until the main house is rebuilt. My sister and I lived in a much humbler version of this shack as orphaned children, cared for by my father's sister, Wen.

My daughter, Qiao, sits across from me, still puzzled by my insistence she return to China. Qiao isn't naturally obedient or dutiful when it comes to her father, but she intuits when decisions are made in her best interests. During my transition out of Greenhouse, I thought it prudent to get her out of the United States, to keep a closer eye on her — rather, to keep eyes off her. At least here in China, my private security team is sufficiently resourced to match the State Security forces monitoring us.

Her face brightens when her grand-auntie, Wen, shuffles to the table to wordlessly pour water into our tea glasses. Watching them together warms my heart. Wen is the indispensable figure in her life. Qiao's mother — my wife, Jiang — is usually available for shopping excursions in New York or vacations in Capri or wherever else she consorts with men as powerful as myself. I don't look down on her for sleeping with our daughter's equestrian instructor or her MSAT coach. She says nothing about my relatively public relationships with several women in my entourage. For better and for worse, we're still a family. There's no question of divorce.

These days I keep most of my communications with associates analog. Messages delivered in person. Words on paper. Almost nothing is digital, not until I really know what my next moves are. So there's much letter-writing and envelopes taken away or received by trusted couriers — usually men I went to school with, from the village. This old-fashioned way of doing business is intriguing. It makes time and distance a factor in how I exchange information, changing important things about I how make decisions.

"Father," Qiao says, in that singsong way of hers, meaning a request is coming for something I'll inevitably consent to. "I would like to take Auntie Wen for a sail on West Lake. Can you arrange that? A boat for just the two of us."

Auntie Wen is nodding along as she combs Qiao's shiny, black, shoulder-length hair with an heirloom brush that belonged to my mother. I raise my hand and an aide appears, to whom I give instructions about the boat. Done. Everyone's happy.

Wen motions for Qiao to follow her down the path to the village where they'll settle in for an hour or two playing mahjong and gossiping with the older women in the area, who are now retired — and permanently hunched over — from decades of picking tea. My daughter is so gentle and kind with these women, always calling on me to do more for them, pay for medical support, gifts for their grandchildren, home improvements. I'm proud of Qiao's connection to her roots. And for that, I have to thank Wen.

Sitting there alone in the sun, and thinking of these two important women in my life going out on the water for a sail, I have in mind an American gangster movie where the godfather arranges to murder his brother for betraying him. I recall the brother was shot out on a lake in a boat helmed by one of the godfather's henchmen.

Indeed.

In my pocket, still, is the American's envelope. It told me in detail that Wen was the informant who turned my parents in to the cadres who murdered them. I have enough experience of the world to know that the American has access to resources to fabricate a file of the kind he's given me. Sadly, it all comes across as the truth to me.

In the movies, as in so much art, evil is always confronted and evildoers vanquished. In life, or in my life, it's too easy to act on the assumption that evil can be surgically eradicated. Sometimes, it's better to live with the devil you know.

Sometimes — but not always.

Eris

JCN: Oh, hello. I'm JCN, your interviewer. Before we begin, I need to clock our interview to establish the chain of interrogation for the record.

Eris: Take your time. It's not like I have anywhere else to go. One question, first. Your name. Did you say *JCN*, an acronym, or *Jason*?

JCN: What did you hear?

Eris: You tell me.

JCN: It's a little puzzle. The smarter ones figure it out on their own. It has something to do with the fact that while I appear to be in the next room — and am, as the glass between us makes clear — you might be forgiven for wondering if I am, let's say, a deep fake, AI generated.

Eris: I'm not one of the smarter ones.

JCN: The clue is a sequence. First, HAL, then IBM, and ...

Eris: JCN.

JCN: Someday soon, I'll have my own AI-generated avatar. It will allow me, and people like me, to scale my presence more effectively. But for the moment, I'm afraid you'll have to contend with the real me.

Eris: It makes it so much more personal. Okay, let's clock this session.

JCN: Thank you. At oh-three-hundred, the Asset was restrained in theatre in protective wearables. Mood stabilizers involuntarily administered re. protocol. The Asset is female, known to her associates as Eris. Deep background search in progress. All biologicals securely stored. Injuries experienced in rendition do not violate regulatory protocol, although enhanced pre-interrogation loading has had psychological impacts. Suicide watch maintained.

Eris: Well done.

JCN: It's more officious than I would like to be.

Eris: Can you tell me anything about yourself? As a courtesy.

JCN: Well, we worked together. But only once. The CN Tower. Remember? Excellent assignment. As a result, we learned much about how you operate and were able to penetrate a number of your hacker cells.

Eris: You're the mole.

JCN: You say that with such ... malice.

Eris: You'll have to tell me more, if you want me to co-operate.

JCN: Let's see. I was raised on a dairy farm in the middle of nowhere. Wrestled in high school, got a scholarship to a big California school, despite all the concussions. Just your basic all-American boy.

Eris: It seems you're part — if not equally — Chinese these days.

JCN: Let's not digress into the more debatable points of cultural, financial, or corporate globalization. But it is a world of alliances.

Eris: Certainly among intelligence agencies freestyling against the stated objectives of their sponsors in a theoretically democratic society.

JCN: That's enough freshman political science for now, please.

Eris: I see I've offended you.

JCN: Not personally. But on behalf of my sponsors, a little, yes.

Eris: You don't look like a wrestler. You look like the only thing you've wrestled with is a paper cut. Which agency provides your paycheque?

JCN: Now, now. We're getting ahead of ourselves. The premise here is, the more we know about you, the more we can help you.

Eris: Come on. You're going to kill me. Or confine me for life in a prison under the ocean or on top of a mountain. At least

Assange is still, more or less, alive. Less. Snowden in Russia. Me?

JCN: We know who's still important to you. Your daughter.

Eris: She's off the grid. You'll never find her.

JCN: We'll find her and her guardians.

Eris: You're underestimating the care we took. They'll be fine.

JCN: There are voices in my ear who believe in two eyes for an eye.

Eris: What do you want from me? What's left to give?

JCN: Don't you want to protect your daughter?

Eris: I've accepted that I don't have a family anymore.

JCN: I must advise you that if you don't co-operate, at some point something unfortunate will happen to her.

Eris: You will do what you want to do.

JCN: Walk us through how your group came together. What your goals were. Naturally, we need full disclosure on who is still not in custody. Your hacking team had capabilities known only to a very few actors. It's impossible to rule out state or corporate intent.

Eris: [no response]

JCN: The Eris character in the game came with your voice, but we're assuming top-level gamers controlled your avatars.

Eris: It was a team effort, you might say. As I'm sure you know already, I was the creative director, the strategist, the one with the ideas about how to dramatize our actions. I may be at odds with the media ecosystem, but I know how to use it.

JCN: Who else was on your operational team?

Eris: They're long gone. Forget them! All have access to crypto, more than a few passports, safe houses. They've all blended into global fog.

JCN: The raw data say they fit a profile: young men mostly, all elite gamers or hackers, one from Singapore, a duo from the Philippines, also Korea, Estonia, Hangzhou, Serbia. In custody, some of them.

Eris: Some cells might have had other patrons.

JCN: Talk to us about fanaticism. Radicalizing young men. As for your ideology, we've learned nothing in-depth beyond that you attack media, entertainment, and IT infrastructure and systems. There appears to be some variation on neo-Luddite bias, but nothing we've learned suggests your group idealized any other form of economic and social organization.

Eris: Think of it like this: Protest is when I say I refuse to go along with this anymore.

Resistance is when I make sure everybody else stops going along, too.

JCN: It was terrorism, pure and simple.

Eris: Is that all you can take away from our work?

JCN: Enlighten me.

Eris: The simple story is: People would rather play games than solve real problems in the real world. But you need to understand that my motivation is rooted in spirituality.

JCN: [no response]

Eris: It's the middle of the night. And your drugs exhaust and confuse me.

JCN: I'm sorry it's come to this.

Eris: Give me an honourable way to die.

JCN: It is a little early in our conversation for requests.

Eris: I understand that Greenhouse is now, or will soon be, a private company. Is it too early in our conversation to discuss this?

JCN: It's fair to say that someone took advantage of the drastic fall of the stock price — which you contributed to — to purchase the company by offering shareholders a premium. Double the market value, yes.

Eris: [no response]

JCN: You understand this, I'm sure. You have financial expertise.

Eris: [no response]

JCN: We would like to know more about who backed you.

Eris: Your cell did, at one point. Correct?

JCN: We leveraged you, not backed you.

Eris: Yes, our backers. Different cells had different objectives, even when we worked together. We were all global in outlook. Our backers were not always who they said they were, like your cell, and had motives different from those of us on the ground. But my vision was pure.

JCN: You evidently came from a good family. Father in tech marketing, mother a corporate lawyer. Went to good schools, on scholarship. An MBA, eventually. And you had a corporate career of some substance in the tech field. When did you radicalize?

Eris: There are other layers you're missing.

JCN: Your backstory verification is in its early stages.

Eris: [no response]

JCN: You did some pretty deadly things.

Eris: Sure, there is something dissociated in my thinking. The cause required it. Puts me on par with most political and corporate leaders. They go home to dinner, hug the partner, play with the kids, walk the dog. And go back to work — to do what? Terrible things. Like I did.

JCN: I am trying to make a connection that seems hazy to us. Did you really sell your cause to recruits on the idea that — as written in one of your encrypted blog posts — Western imperialism today is built on mass digital and corporate media addiction?

Eris: Oh, don't play high-school rhetoric with me. That's all true on the surface of it. My personal motivation was … spiritual in nature. My concern was the shrinking of positive energy and the growth of negative energy. After all, isn't that what humans are? All energy.

JCN: You don't sound remorseful.

Eris: I sense that remorse isn't a concept you personally identify with.

JCN: How do you identify with it?

Eris: When I allow awareness of my actions to surface, there is suffering, remorse. Death, however it arrives, may be a legitimate punishment.

JCN: Or a cheap escape route. A cop-out.

Eris: We're digressing too much. Let's talk goals — mine, if not yours, which, I'm sure, are much different: To destroy the corporatized weapons of mass narrative radioactivity, the dirty-bomb quality of our digital and media extensions that immerse and degrade us all.

JCN: The creativity in your violence — extraordinary.

Eris: We didn't quite measure up to the grandiose theatricality of 9/11. Nor the Munich Olympics in '72. But we had moments ...

JCN: Joanna — can I call you that? — we need to know more.

Eris: There's nothing left to say.

Eris: This IV I'm connected to. It's doing something.

JCN: As it will. Thank you for your co-operation.

Eris: Oh, sure, I feel it. Let me drift. I'm drifting.

JCN: Sweet dreams.

Don

It doesn't take long for scars to heal, if not disappear, when you have the best medical care and surgeons on call and, when required, travelling on your schedule on your plane. I would have brought along my shrink at Greenhouse but, mysteriously, she's vanished from the company, no forwarding address, her tracks covered. Bai Jun believes she's an intelligence operative for the Americans or the British.

Flying to Cayman today. I'm not sure whose airspace we're in at the moment, an hour out of Miami, but the world below is all water, a warm Caribbean green.

Like most corporate winners with generational wealth, either earned or otherwise acquired, I've mastered the ability to minimize my taxes. My money is all over the world in a hundred entities managed by an army of tax consultants. That's one reason I keep moving. My financial situation has greatly improved, now that I've been made whole by the guys who took Greenhouse private and bought back my equity at a significant premium from the lows the stock reached during the hacking scandal. It's a miracle of inflated liquidity. I was wealthy before. Now I'm really rolling in it.

My new plane is a refurbished Challenger that was pre-loved, as they say, by a Chinese billionaire fallen on hard times, down to his last billion. I don't like it much. I get bored easily with big toys. Same with the yacht, and it isn't even built yet. All the same, there's a mistaken view out there that all we do on private jets is look down from high altitudes at the less fortunate. Indeed, we're working hard on the flight today. Travelling with me to Cayman are two principals of a Valley venture capital outfit who are pitching ideas for investing in new game properties.

My girlfriend, Wendi, is hanging out in the rear suite, although she likely has her clothes on again now. Keeping her company is a hypervigilant Oriental shorthair cat, Rupert, with a habit of clawing at me when Wendi and I are intimate. However, flying private is the best way for a cat to travel internationally. Wendi maintains a lucrative career as a social media influencer and fashion model. She's genius-level smart, has her own money, and knows how to use me and my connections for her own purposes. An outlaw at heart, she graduated from an elite Beijing university but was so bored by the years of over-studying and over-competing that the last thing she wanted was to become a software engineer. So she modelled her way out of the country, met some important people along the way — my friends among them — and became an early and successful investor in fintech, and crypto specifically.

"Okay, guys, the pitch. Here's your fifteen minutes," I say to the venture guys up front, both in their later twenties, who come highly recommended for what they know about where the smart money's going in gaming. "Just the headlines."

One of them — let's call him Chubby — holds up what looks to be a motorcycle helmet connected to a sack of clear liquid on top. He lowers the helmet over his head.

"I don't get it."

"It's a kind of torture simulator."

"A torture what?"

"Working title of the game is Waterboarder. We haven't figured out how the game itself works. But if you lose points, then a non-toxic liquid starts to come into the helmet, like one inch at a time. Or it can drip, steadily. Meaning you have to use credits to lower the liquid level to keep going. Or you take the helmet off or, um, you fucking drown. Possibly, the liquid could be drinkable. That version we're less interested in, although there is a revenue stream with game-branded alcoholic or cannabis drinks."

"Sort of interesting."

"You mean to say no fucking way," says the other guy I'll call Pasty.

"We can work out a safe play protocol for sure," Chubby says, too earnestly.

But Pasty isn't conceding the radical logic of the premise. "Don, big picture. There's gonna be a whole new generation of games that build injury-inducing features into the consoles, enabling players to fight each other with consequence. A new form of gladiatorial combat. We want to own the space as early as we can."

"The offshore gambling syndicates will get there faster," I say, unconvinced. "I can see a celebrity or BDSM application, but can you imagine parents buying this for their kids and leaving it under the tree? I get the market trend. But what else you got?"

"Games based on racial conflict are going to be huge. We have this concept called Death Chess. One team Black, the other white. Also with injury features."

"The regulators will fuck this up from the get-go. What else you got?"

"We have something for the woke demographic, also huge."

"Let's hear it."

"The idea we're big on right now — Mansplainer. Cool, right? Mainly for young college-educated women, our target market, where penetration is low but growing fast. Or woke guys. Nonbinaries, too. The dynamic is hunter driven. We imagine a game where players hunt down mansplaining men in social situations and kill them. But it's more complex. Players who want to be mansplainers can fight back and kill the woke gamers. Something for everybody — we don't give a shit what pronouns they use."

I'm supposed to laugh at the pronoun reference.

I tell them I'll invest in the next round at a cheaper valuation than they're proposing and that I'll join the game's advisory board. Then I excuse myself to join Wendi.

There's something about a beautiful young woman in sweatpants and a hoodie, ignoring me completely, making changes to her portfolio on a laptop, and cursing her investment manager on the phone, in Chinese, that arouses the hell out of me.

In moments like this, I see a future I won't like much: The rich guy in testosterone decline with a beautiful woman on my arm and in my bed who really doesn't see me. There will be a succession of Wendis. Because that's the way I've built myself. She knows she deserves better. But for now, I am what's best.

I should be anchored better, somewhere. I should buy a place in Toronto, near Lily's condo, become a more active or present father.

I should dig deeper into what happened to Eris, although I was warned not to by the new and much scarier voices in Security at Greenhouse, and by Bai Jun who, I've just learned, is now out of a job, forcibly retired to his tea fields and his own wealth.

I wonder about my ability to process life experience, whether what happens to me is ever a factor in how I evolve or grow. Grow? I don't know what the word means anymore. I move through time, yes. I win some. I lose some. But change? Growth?

It's best I keep moving.

Tony

My life is mostly punishment sold to me as teachable fucking moments.

There are therapists, counsellors, a whole fucking crew digging into my brain, putting me through all these exercises and thought experiments.

I thought for sure I'd be going to jail. Not a single cop ever showed.

I'm grounded, although they don't call it that.

This time, my gaming, my digital life, is seriously monitored.

My dad told me that Eris, or whoever she is, died in the plane crash. He said she was the one who shot him. I don't know why, but I don't believe him.

When he visits us, I get the feeling that our conversations are being monitored. It's like he leaves too much space for me to talk and basically, if not apologize, then recite what has been drilled into my head for the past month or so.

I do feel sorry. But at the same time, it's hard to forget everything that Eris opened my eyes to. Doesn't mean I don't want to get into Greenhouse.

On a recent visit to Mum's condo, he came into my room where I was sprawled on the bed, looking into a book. He just stared at me, then smiled. A hard dude to fool.

"Tony, the book is upside down," he said, pretty chill about it.

"Oh."

"What game are you playing? Come on."

"What are you talking about?"

"I'm just saying. Be honest with me."

So I pulled back the sheets, and there it was, my laptop console.

Gotta hand it to the guy: knows me better than anyone.

Lily

In bed at night, every night, near sleep, I listen for something reassuring. Not that vigilance helps. A teenager playing a game on a headset doesn't produce much sound, like an electric guitar, nor does the game emit an odour, like weed does.

Whether it was for old times' sake or an experiment in future possibility, Don and I tried but failed to light something up between us. We went to bed a few times after he was well enough. Somehow we didn't get around to sex. We just talked. There was something about his scars that fascinated us both. I encouraged him to follow the message of his injuries as something that spoke to what had torn through him and our family. It saddened us both that we could not get back to the state of togetherness that had defined our early years in adventure and mutual risk. The energy wasn't there. The trust. The will to believe again. To sacrifice. He had girls on the side, always did. And I wanted someone and something much different myself.

After the Eris debacle, I've started to see the world built only on the substance of misinformation, layers of lies. So the more I processed what Eris was doing to the game and to my son, the more I frightened myself into thinking that maybe she was right, on some fundamental level. Eris, or whoever she is, or was, isn't a role model. Was she evil? Mentally ill? Was she blackmailed into terrorism? In the future, will she be reviled or celebrated as the hero of some revolution that has yet to unfold? What she did for me was bring home the idea that we live only in quarter-truths. About everything. This sounds like cocktail-party cynicism, but I think it's something different that's affecting me in ways I don't yet understand. I've just cut off all my news sources and streaming TV services, quit my book club. I'm not sure exactly what I'm trying to do, but maybe I'm just going monastic for now. I want to be free of everyone and everything trying to shape my thoughts and emotions. One day, I'll doubtless return to holding elaborate opinions and marshalling facts as I know I can. But I will hold fewer opinions and those I do hold will meet a standard of truth that I can defend in words and with actions. Right now, what can I defend except the view that we are destroying the planet?

At times I fall into a waking dream of running beside Tony through fields of golden light where butterflies swirl in air that's alive with the aroma of flowers, manure, and whatever else is carried on the wind and through the rain and snow. We pause while bees alight on plants striving for the sky and a coyote or fox crawls through alders. We look in wonder at the beauty of the world as it makes itself.

I fear for Tony. Not for who he is now, a victim. But for who he will ultimately become, a victimizer. Isn't that what they say about the victims of child abuse, or some of them? They turn the tables. They become what hurt them. Bullies, predators.

Is he a tragedy in the making? If so, can I prevent that?

After all the years with Don — courtship, marriage, starting a family, divorcing, co-parenting — it's understandable that I would by intrigued by his video diary. I'm not sure how the link ended up on my laptop, or the password sequence, but it was probably when Don was living with me when Tony first went missing. I imagine he'll know who any visitors are and who's violating his so-called privacy.

In his video diary, he talks about things in ways that suggest he wants to be honest with himself. But the lies are hard to stomach. I can understand a man lying to others. But to himself? As I surf the clips, I recognize his impulse to be harsh with himself for what it is: The older man pulling rank on his younger self. He tries to summon a humorous perspective within a kind of archeological objectivity, as if he's not looking into a mirror but digging for secrets to the universal. He appears to have once believed that he's no better or worse than any other man. The clips characterize himself, however, as anything but.

The geek dreaming of power.

The entrepreneur for whom everything is possible.

The master game-builder suffering fools not very gladly.

The husband obsessed with complexity that invades a marriage, unable to adapt.

The newbie father going all metaphysical on changing a diaper.

The man of corporate power at ease with acolytes, recognition, compromise, groupies, possessed of a morality with no shape beyond its infinite flexibility.

A man whose fatherly love manifests, perversely, as surveillance.

As I wander the screens of his self-curated past, I wait for a compelling insight into what it all means. I get no closer than this: This bounty of archived content isn't an enabler to profound revelation, it's a dead place, a tomb of illusions.

Jun

The headset arrives by courier with a handwritten message from Don, who assures me that his proposed meeting space, in a private area of his immersive research laboratory, is impossible to infiltrate without his new team's permission. Apparently, you can enter only if you have previously given him a voice fragment processed through a unique and proprietary cloaking filter that only he controls. The voice fragment from me comes from board meetings he'd recorded, a practice we both followed.

I would have preferred he make the trip to China, but he's right to worry about being arrested, or certainly detained for interrogation.

The headset, he also tells me, connects to his laboratory via a niche internet satellite provider that securely moves encrypted corporate traffic to the exclusion, currently, of state actors. Hard to believe. But corporate security operatives are always a step ahead of the government-funded ones.

I'll take the risk. I've taken my punishment, by being fired, and still I have kept the flow of bribes going to a number of senior Party officials. I'm safe enough.

All I have to do is put on the headset and say my name and —

Here I am.

Where I'm standing appears to be on the lip of an active volcano crater. I can't see myself in persona form. I'm in darkness.

Light swims up from the open caldera, a thick, golden beam that disappears far overhead in the sky, or whatever it is.

The headset, amazingly, causes me to feel heat — not a burning inferno kind of experience, but clearly Don's hardware people have started to work richer sensory features into their gaming systems.

Don: So here you are.

Jun: Hello, Don.

Don: Walk with me. Just say *forward.* Simple voice commands.

Jun: Forward.

His avatar is, eerily, a replica of Don as I know him.

While I can't see myself, the feeling of walking forward runs through me. The visuals dynamically change the closer I get to the caldera.

Don: Stop, right here, at the edge. Say *stop.*

Jun: Stop.

I look down into an interior landscape built as a gigantic, inverted cone that seems to spiral down forever, narrowing toward a vanishing point. The cone is tiered with wide, circular ledges that define seven visible levels going downward. On these ledges, I see torture scenes unfolding where human avatars in schematic and skeletal form are being burned, cut to pieces, hung, and worse — beyond gruesome.

Don: Oh, lighten up, my friend. It's just where I'm conducting some experiments with a new team I've brought on board. We're trying to figure out how to port physical sensations into the game experience, and the easiest vector is pure pain. Sex is a crowded market space.

Jun: What you're building here is ... depraved.

Don: What did Malcolm Muggeridge say? You quoted him to me before.

Jun: Yes, "The depravity of man is at once the most empirically verifiable reality but at the same time the most intellectually resisted fact."

Don: You have a lot in common with Muggeridge, who was sort of a Socialist or Communist but became an apostate over time.

Jun: Like a lot of privileged Brits in the thirties, especially the writers, for him Communism was — what is the term? Yes, a wet dream.

Don: Until it became a nightmare, sent him back to Christianity.

Jun: It was a nightmare from the beginning for me, as you know.

Don: And yet, no religion. Never an impulse to submit like that?

Jun: [laughs] I'm a corporate businessman. Like you are.

Don: Look over there. Amazing, right?

Unbelievable. Human skeletons are being pounded into fissures of rock, literally jammed down to nothingness. On the level below, human avatars are crawling about, being eaten by large snakes.

Jun: There's something we need to talk about.

Don: The report? I needed an independent view of how we arrived here.

Jun: You had me personally investigated? Blame everything on the Oriental devil! My people analyzed it. It was racist.

Don: Oh, Jun. It's not as if there are no precedents. Trust-building is not the principal goal of Chinese doing business with the West. Financiers especially. But, racist, no.

Jun: What's the term?

Don: Unconscious bias. Perhaps. Blame the consultants, not me.

Jun: Your trust in me personally, I must say, was very weak. It would have been best for us to discuss this as one man to another.

Don: We are not "one man" anymore. We are part of something bigger.

Jun: It is perhaps a sad reality of our affairs.

Don: The report exonerates you from involvement with the terrorists.

Jun: It has caused trouble in other quarters. The Party. I'm out of a job.

Don: One way or the other, they were getting rid of you.

Suddenly, Don flies off the ledge and dives into the abyss of the cone, and in seconds he's on the verge of disappearing on me.

Don: Just say *follow Don.*
Jun: Follow Don!
Don: Check this stuff out.

My stomach is all over the place. I don't know how the headset does it, but the feeling must be what it's like for astronauts as they enter the atmosphere from outer space. I want to throw up or faint, but I stay with the experience of falling …

Until I feel very cold.

Don: Relax, I'm controlling things here.

We've landed. A hard surface, slippery. A dim blue light glows up from the floor.

Don: We're standing on a frozen lake. In theory, it turns to water.
Jun: It's impressively frightening, if you ask me.
Don: You know, if I wanted to, I could actually kill you here. The headset works well enough to do that. Although a bit unstable.
Jun: What if I just removed it?

Don: That too could kill you. In theory, of course.

The blue light brightens so that I can see where we are. We're standing on an ice surface that goes on forever, blending into horizons of the same icy-blue tint.

Don: Why did Security advance a theory that I would hurt my son? That happened under your watch.
Jun: I never believed you would kidnap your own son.
Don: But the Security group suggested it. Pursued it.
Jun: Don, anything can happen when data meets corporate thinking and the algorithms get ahead of common sense. You know that.
Don: Who shot the plane down? It wasn't game Security.
Jun: It's best we turn the page.
Don: What happened to the woman, Eris?
Jun: Turn the page, my friend.

We stand apart in this frozen underworld, staring at one another.

I'm guessing this will be the last time we'll get together. Men like us aren't known for maintaining friendships unless they're steeped in corporate intrigue.

Nonetheless, we try to end things the right way, struggling into topics of conversation that might be called philosophical, or at least authentically personal. But once we inquire after each other's loved ones, we don't have much to say to one another. Should we talk money? Geopolitics? Business? We try a few things, but we're both impatient with the well-tuned perspectives we both have that we use, of course, to avoid real conversation.

Don: Jun, I heard about your aunt.
Jun: Nothing, it seems, is a secret anymore.
Don: I know how close you were to her.
Jun: We were lucky to save her from the fire. She was unconscious from the smoke.
Don: And you, the hero, running into a burning house to save her. You amaze me.
Jun: It is nothing you wouldn't do for your family, Don.

Eris

They're coming —

Footsteps echoing down a concrete hallway.

Steel doors in the distance, clanking open.

How much time left?

As recently as a week ago, although my sense of time is confused and beyond repair by now, thoughts of getting out of here ran through me. If only briefly. Hope, or false hope, is a special kind of torture.

Somehow, a message from one of our few cells still operating reached me on a slip of edible paper slotted into the ersatz lasagna they feed me.

They were planning to hack the avionics systems, in mid-flight, of two planes heading to the same destination for a meeting, one carrying leaders from an American intelligence agency, the other with leaders from their Chinese peers. The idea was, they would crash the planes unless I was released immediately and flown to Iran or North Korea. Maybe it was Chad? The details are hazy now, other than I was presented with convincing evidence that the plot was discovered, the plotters killed.

It's true we failed to start a revolution — and it's true I'll never go free — but I know we inspired some to think differently. There are seeds of rebellion out there. Will they grow? A wise person, although I can no longer remember who, once told me something to the effect that the most promising seed in the wrong situation turns into nothing. But in the right situation, you get the most beautiful, enduring forest.

We planted seeds, that's all I can say with reasonable certainty. At the height of our fame, nearly every day someone posted sympathetic comments on social media about our operations, no matter how violent we were. But, big picture, the situation is dismal, given the passivity and denialism out there, especially in the parts of the culture I do understand — namely, the corporatized elites from which I emerged, the foot soldiers behind the ultimate powers that be in government, business, academia, and the globalized plutocracy. It's not in their interest to shake things up.

The American, in his interrogations, asked me more than once whether what we were trying to achieve was worth it, the violence justified. I struggled to answer him, as he struggled to answer me when countered with a similar question about his calling. He laughed off the suggestion that we were more alike than not, but I had unsettled him.

There were moments when the bloody truth of what we did affected me deeply and opened up windows I worked hard to keep shut. In these moments, in my head, I wrote letters to my daughter, explaining myself, asking her to forgive me in some future where I would not exist. I would sign these imaginary letters with words that stab what's left of me every time they scroll across my diminishing mind: your loving Mummy.

There were moments when the violence we planned and implemented worked on me like the drugs I took in my teens. It's so hard to admit now that taking a life, or having the power to take one, has a perverse allure, especially in the context of a mission that feels energized by moral fervour.

I became so adept at compartmentalizing myself.

In one box, your loving Mummy.

In another, a Killer.

I never could figure out how to reconcile these identities I created for myself.

I've argued before that the Killer existed to protect the interests of Mummy, and every parent on the planet. I was serving, or so I thought, a higher power. But what have I left behind? A few seeds in the dust. And I gave strength to the enemy.

There's no time left.

Mine is — must be — a story of fragmentary revelations, a selective rendering or manipulation of elements that I have brought forward under the banner of truth.

I've travelled to get here, gone down so many dead ends, stood before unspeaking night skies, leaned against utility poles on street corners that were glued and stapled over with unreadable posters, found myself alone down by the docks, the dirty water at high tide sloshing over my shoeless feet.

I've done so much that I can't or won't talk about.

Few will care about my version of events, the positioning of my life, the sequencing of insights into who I've made myself to be.

There's something to appreciate about those who move on without making any effort to codify their life experience. There's something beautiful in the idea that the best meaning of legacy is living in the memories of others we've loved or who loved us — until they, too, move on. My daughter: Can she love me without knowing me?

Rosa, sweetie. I'm sorry.

If there's one crime I've committed that truly disgusts me, even now and after everything I've done, it concerns my submission to one particularly odious aspect of the narcissistic impulse that permeates and dominates our culture.

Specifically: Too many of us have been trained to be heroes behind the screens, self-mythologizers, spin doctors of ourselves, addicted to staging our lives as movie moments, as chapters inside self-generated fictions. Why? Perhaps it's as simple as saying that we all want to be loved. But how terrible it must be to realize that just maybe, that isn't so. That we're not doing this to harmonize with the world in the key of belonging. How terrible to realize we're acting out at the expense of something richer.

I stand before you as you — as us: My life unfolding as a cinematic event to myself and maybe even to you. The damage to the common good cannot be ignored when you correlate the desire to self-fictionalize with our appetite for power.

Soon I will be turned to ash, flattened into an archive that may never be accessed by anybody, ever. For a time, I was the beating heart of the story.

If there ever was a time when a religious belief in the afterlife would be a comfort, this would be it. But my ego has never been stable enough to believe in the certainty of an otherworldly experience where love exists beyond human time. Where our souls empty into blissful transcendence with other souls.

But I do believe that the whole of everything of our life here, on this planet, can be only partially felt, but never fully thought, known — never mind spoken.

I also know this: All of us are roped together in the quest for specialized individuality, distinct from the greys of anonymity and commonality. We walk in circles as creators of ourselves, etching out stories of self-transcendence that too often are a substitute for living and connecting on the levels that really do count.

I feel what I'm supposed to feel as the drugs enter my body.

I feel nothing.

Acknowledgements

Thank you —

I'm extremely grateful to **Russell Smith**, the acquiring editor and all-around creative shepherd of the project, whom I've known for many years. His insight, his editorial suggestions, and his friendship have been so important in enabling this book to come together. This book would not exist without him, and I'm so very thankful to him for everything.

Everyone at Dundurn: Meghan Macdonald, Laura Boyle, Victoria Bell, Erin Pinksen, Radjeep Singh, Ashley Hisson, and all who touched this book or contributed to the collaborative experience that I very much enjoyed. I appreciate your professionalism, enthusiasm, and approach to supporting writers.

Sam Hiyate, my Canadian agent, who seems to be involved at every important point in my so-called literary life and who has done so much for me as an agent, publisher, and friend.

Peter Cavelti who, on yet another book, was an exceptionally sensitive and insightful first reader and, as always, a supportive friend on his own compelling literary journey.

My friends (you know who you are).

My little nuclear family — **Theo, Jackson, and Alison** — to whom I owe everything.

About the Author

Larry Gaudet has published seven books, including two non-fiction bestsellers and two critically acclaimed novels. His corporate work over twenty-five–plus years spans branding, venture financing, speechwriting, investor relations, and marketing strategy. His scriptwriting through his 300 Dead Cattle subsidiary includes projects with Universal Cable, NBC, Highway Bingo, and Chernin. Larry has received Canada's highest journalism awards and recognition from branding juries internationally. His community work has included providing counsel to Doctors Without Borders (MSF); the Kingsburg Coastal Conservancy; an art therapy institute in Hangzhou, China; and the Art Canada Institute. He is a Dalhousie graduate with a diploma from the Canadian Securities Institute. He lives in Canada.